Kala's Choice

MARCIA BREECE

Publishing Partners

Books By Marcia Breece

Finding This Place:
One Woman's Journey Beyond Restriction

Secrets Lost:
Secrets Remembered

Kala's Choice

Publishing Partners
Port Townsend, WA
www.publishing-partners.com

This is a work of fiction. Names, characters, businesses, places, and events are either the products of the author's imagination or used in a fictitious manner. Any resemblance to actual persons, living or dead, or actual events is purely coincidental.

Printed in the United States of America

Library of Congress Number 2016918323

ISBN: 978-1-944887-16-2
eISBN:978-1-944887-17-9

gratitude

Thanks to my dear friends, Kimberly King and Ken Grantham, for helping this book materialize. Once again they patiently endured character-sharing *long* before the story developed. I am grateful for their patience and support in the early stages.

Thanks to Sheila Bender, Molly Hollenbach and Tess Taft who offered coaching and editing, each with her own set of skills, insight, knowledge, and ability to provide powerful feedback.

Thanks also to beta readers Patricia Lennox, Ruth Lytle, and Karen Watts for providing valuable feedback to help the story come alive.

dedication

To feral children
Now is all they know.
Love is all they have.

chapter 1

Mumbai India—1994

Kala nursed her new-born son. His tiny, demanding mouth brought tears of pain as if, at two days old, he knew his place in her life. Once satisfied, he slept. Kala changed his diaper, swaddled him in a soft blue blanket, and placed him in the bassinet.

Dim light cast grotto-like curves on her narrow face while she carefully draped a yellow silk sari in the Punjabi style her grandmother had taught her. When her eyes fell on her daughter, Devi, Kala smiled, revealing for a moment the radiate beauty smothered by her arranged marriage.

Staring without focus, Kala plaited her long black hair while a silver barrette waited between her teeth. Engraved on the back with Kala's birth date and name, it was a gift from her grandmother. Kala believed the barrette protected her, as if imbued with Amma's loving energy. She secured the end of her braid with the silver ornament as she had done for as long as she could remember.

Devi opened her honey-gold eyes as Kala slipped a red embroidered party dress over her head. The three year old's bright eyes filled the room with happiness. The child smiled but made no sound. She had learned not to wake her father in the next room.

Kala and her husband, Atal, lived in a mansion in Mumbai, owned by the Achara family since the English left India in the 1940s. Atal's brother also lived in the mansion with his wife and young sons. All three men were government officials with power over the privileged as well as the indigent. Although they had well-paying government jobs, the bulk of their income came from graft. Kala's husband, the oldest, was nearly as gray as his father. They were tall for Indian men, with copper skin, fairer than most, and a strong family resemblance. Their bushy hair sprung like unruly garden weeds. Menacing ebony eyes revealed the cruelty they were each capable of, but Atal's eyes were golden and even more sinister than his brother's.

Kala's father had arranged the marriage as a business favor to the Achara family. They treated the beautiful bride as they would a worthless bauble, not with cruelty, but with total lack of love, respect, or devotion. Kala gave birth to a five-pound girl nine months after the wedding. Atal and his parents blamed Kala for the unfortunate result. A girl.

From the day she gave birth, Kala walked with Devi in the vast fragrant garden and often napped with the baby on a blanket under an arch of passion flower vines. The girl, small for her age, learned to walk on soft, manicured grass. Kala taught Devi Punjabi words for mama, hello, and bye-bye as well as names of the fruits and vegetables.

Although he never struck her, Atal crudely mounted Kala every night, not with passion but with duty. He rolled off as if finishing an unpleasant dental appointment, and rarely spoke to her again until the next coupling. He slept in his own room. When she gave birth to a son a few days after Devi's birthday, Atal was pleased. He dyed his gray hair to look like a younger new father. "Now I have a boy child, get rid of that girl. Leave her at the orphanage!" he commanded, as if Devi were a worn-out plastic toy.

Kala knew he husband's cruelty all too well. One day she had walked by the kitchen just as her mother-in-law's arm swept through the air and splattered kerosene onto Kala's fat, irritating, sister-in-law. Blood chilling screams and the smell of roasting flesh filled the hallway.

"We-must-call-for-help," said the mother-in-law, in a monotonal, unconcerned voice, and she dragged pregnant Kala away from the burning body. As the screams subsided, Atal appeared with buckets of water and put out the fire. The tiled kitchen sustained little damage, but the demanding young mother was dead. Kala saw her husband nod, as a smile rose between the old woman and her son. Now they would find a new bride for Atal's brother and demand a huge dowry.

There was no investigation.

Like a stealth leopard stalking its prey, Kala slipped through the mansion and into the yard with her sleeping daughter on her hip. Her yellow sari and Devi's red dress glowed as she hurried along the illuminated path to the street. The exotic tropical garden and a tall stone wall protected the property from the palm-lined boulevard ordinarily teeming with cars, scooters and auto-rickshaws. At this hour only an occasional taxi passed. The intense perfume of passion flower blossoms filled the air. Kala paused. She hoped the fruity, floral fragrance would evoke loving memories, and Devi would know how much Kala loved her. She pressed her lips to Devi's forehead.

The opulent wrought iron gate cried like a hungry kitten when they squeezed through. The barrette at the end of her braid flashed with the last glimmer of light as the black metal winked shut. Kala hurried beyond the wall that had safeguarded Devi from the harsh realities of Mumbai. As the fragrant air soured, the echo of her husband's voice reminded her, *Leave her at the orphanage!*

Kala walked for hours, burying her face in her daughter's soft hair and gulping the musky toddler sweetness. Kala's pace quickened through an alley teeming with fat, fearless rats. She hurried beyond the menacing stone wall where a concealed postern window and worn bamboo basket accepted *donations* inconspicuously.

She knew, once inside, no child escaped the orphanage.

She moved aimlessly through dark alleys, passing lavish hotels and putrid slums. As midnight blue replaced the utter blackness of night, she all but stumbled over a pack of children sleeping like a litter of puppies near a fruit-*wallah's* cart.

One of the older children rested her arm over a smaller child. Another spooned against her back. Kala sensed a yellow glow of love among the pack of orphans. The love she sought for her daughter.

Her choice was suddenly clear.

Hunching like a heron in the shadows, Kala unhooked the front closure of her yellow *choli* and offered her breast. The child suckled until milk trickled from her lips. Kala used her *pallu* to wipe the sleeping child's lips. Taking the barrette from the end of her own braid she squeezed it in her fist as she had when she was a child. She said a prayer to her grandmother, "Amma, please keep Devi safe for I cannot." She fastened the barrette into her daughter's hair.

Hugging Devi as close to her naked breast as possible, she knelt to place the toddler on the sidewalk, next to the oldest girl. Careful not to wake the other children, Kala lifted the sleeping girl's arm and let it lay over her three year old's red dress.

With her palms pressed together, she silently blessed the small family of orphans and then, she walked away.

Filled with grief beyond tears, scarcely breathing, she forgot to re-hook her *choli*, leaving only the *pallu* to cover her round, milk-swollen breasts.

Yellow chiffon glowed around her like a flickering flame about to blow out. When she came to the Arabian Sea, she kept walking toward the rim of the world until the unfolding sari floated above her like a full moon's reflection.

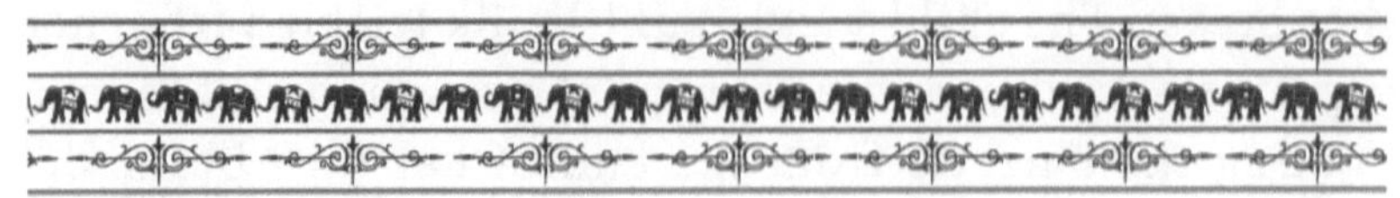

chapter 2

RADEEKA

Raj Khawaja earned an MD at Mumbai University Medical School, completed five years of surgical residency at Stanford in America, and received a PhD in biomedical engineering at Harvard. He returned to Mumbai to marry Ruchi. They had fallen in love as undergrads. Raj was tall, with slim hips and a barrel chest. Ruchi's head almost reached his square jaw. Both easily volunteered a big white grin. Neither had living family. Theirs was a love marriage.

An upper-middle class couple, they lived in a condo on the tenth floor of a high rise overlooking Chowpatty Beach and the Arabian Sea. Their spacious flat had a Western-style kitchen, living room and two bedrooms with ensuite bathrooms, all facing the horizon where saffron sunsets melted into the sea.

After the wedding, Raj took a job selling ambulatory blood pressure monitors, pacemakers, and other devices to hospitals and clinics all over Asia. A talented surgeon in his own right, Raj often demonstrated during actual surgeries, instructing students and doctors on the use of pacemakers and other devices. The sales position was far more lucrative than any medical practice in Mumbai and he felt he was giving back when he had the opportunity to teach at universities and hospitals.

Raj especially enjoyed working with Dr. Keir Keefe and his students in Mumbai. Dr. Keefe's lack of ego made the work enjoyable. Dr. Keefe had a keen understanding of the challenges facing the population of Mumbai. Raj invited Keir to dinner on several occasions and Ruchi enjoyed his charm and pleasant sense of humor.

On their first anniversary, which fell during the Ganesh festival, Raj arranged for the delivery of his gift to Ruchi. Three shirtless men struggled off the elevator with a heavy wooden crate. Inside, a brass idol of Ganesh, the elephant headed god of new beginning and wisdom, stood more than a meter tall. The three moving men struggled to place the idol inside the flat by the front door.

The idol's elephant ears were wide and his trunk curved out and down. His right palm blessed everyone that passed while his left held fruit. Ruchi hugged Raj. "Thank you, dear husband."

A year later, their daughter was born during the Ganesh festival. Raj cradled his newborn in his arms, smelling her hair and nuzzling her soft cheek. Only a few hours old, the infant peered into her father's eyes and melted his heart.

He brought her home with a proud grin and introduced the tiny newborn to the doorman and his wife, Mr. and Mrs. Hamadani. "We will call her Radeeka," he told them as he curled over the tiny bundle like a penguin protecting his chick.

"My good father was much older than my mother and died when I was twelve," Raj told Mr. Hamadani. "He left a considerable inheritance and instructions for my uncle so that my mother and I would be safe. He bought this building to produce income and ensure that I could be educated in America. Because of his advanced age, he knew he would not survive to see it. I have the same plan for Radeeka," he smiled down at Ruchi standing at his elbow, "but we have no living blood relatives. I would like you and your wife to look after my wife and daughter if anything should happen to me."

"We would be most honored," said Mr. Hamadani, bowing his head.

"Of course, we would be honored," said Mrs. Hamadani, wagging her hijab-covered head and reaching out to hold the baby, "but do not speak of such things."

"Still," said Raj, supporting her little head as he released his daughter into Mrs. Hamadani's arms for the first time, "I will sleep well knowing that Radeeka will always be loved and cared for if I'm not here to enjoy her life."

Mr. Hamadani was shorter than Ruchi. His own wife was even smaller, with skin much lighter than her husband's. They had grown up Muslim in the valleys of Kashmir, enjoying a rural life, but escaped to Mumbai when conflict escalated and militant revolutionaries invaded their quiet farming village.

Raj and Ruchi never told Radeeka about their plans for her if something should happen. She was too young, but they made sure Radeeka knew that Mr. and Mrs. Hamadani loved her. Mrs. Hamadani cared for Radeeka when Raj and Ruchi went out for the evening or when Ruchi went shopping. Mr. Hamadani told long, happy stories of his childhood in the mountains of Kashmir while she sat on the marble floor by his desk hugging her knees. When she got older he welcomed her home with hugs and sweets after school.

Mr. Hamadani and his wife were only a few years older than Raj and Ruchi. They all loved each other like brothers and sisters, aunt and uncle, despite their religious differences.

Most Indian men wanted a boy child but Raj was thrilled to have a daughter. He read to her every day, in English, Hindi, and Marathi. Raj and Ruchi spoke both Hindi and English at home. As soon as Radeeka could walk, they flew kites together in the park by the sea. Radeeka's high-pitched giggles and Raj's deep laughter drifted together like the kite's tail twisting in the salty tropical breeze.

On weekends, Raj, Ruchi and Radeeka enjoyed picnics on the beach with their feet in the hot sand. Every June they watched storms gather, bringing the monsoon season along with cooler air.

Before Radeeka was five years old, Raj taught her the value of money. "Always have coins in your pockets," Raj told Radeeka. "You never know when you might be needing a coin." When she walked to school or played with her friends, her little pockets jingled.

Ruchi wore western-style clothes except on special occasions, and dressed her daughter in jeans and Old Navy t-shirts like America school girls. Together they worshiped Hindu gods. She often took Radeeka's face in her hands and kissed her forehead and both cheeks, "Always be grateful to Lord Ganesh, Radeeka my sweet. He is the god of success and good fortune. The elephant god has blessed our family with prosperity and love." As Radeeka grew, she and her mother stood in front of the four-foot brass idol before they left the flat and again when they returned. Over the years, their daily touch buffed the curve of his trunk to a bright shine while the rest glowed with a radiant patina.

On Tuesday afternoons, Raj, Ruchi, and Radeeka dressed in traditional Indian attire, Raj often in his dark blue *pajama kurta*, and Ruchi in her favorite green and blue *sari*. They said puja at the Temple of Ganesh in their native Marathi language and made offerings of fruit, ladoos, modakas or dhruva grass. After a day of fasting in honor of Lord Ganesh, they ate rice, dahl, and naan at their favorite restaurant.

Raj made a weekly deposit of rupees in the orphanage's donaxtion basket. The hinges squeaked as he opened the little postern gate. "We are very lucky Radeeka, my sweet," Raj said in Marathi, "We must help less fortunate people."

For five years it was their Tuesday tradition. Raj lifted Radeeka so she could drop rupees into the basket, but she buried her face on her father's shoulder.

Radeeka grew tall enough to reach the basket herself, but she still hid behind her father. "I do not like this place, Papa," Radeeka cried. Switching from Marathi to English, "Carry me, Papa. Carry me." She sensed the harsh edge of sorrow oozing from beyond the stone wall.

🐘 🐘 🐘

One evening, Radeeka sat on a stool, with her chin resting on the vanity, watching her mother get ready for a party. Ruchi edged her eyes with thin black lines, brushed dark green shadow on her eyelids, lengthened her lashes with mascara and rubbed crimson *sindoor* powder into her center-parted jet-black hair.

"What is that?" said Radeeka.

"This red powder in my hair tells the world I am married to your papa," she smiled, pinching Radeeka's chin with her red fingers, "but the powder can't tell them how much we love him, can it?" Ruchi rinsed the powder from her fingertips and released the drain. Radeeka shivered as the red water swirled in the white sink.

Ruchi wrapped herself in an elegant royal blue sari with gold embroidery. Layers of gold bracelets jangled up her brown arms and sparkled like her eyes.

Raj and Ruchi were attending an event to celebrate Raj's latest promotion. "Your father and I are going out for dinner tonight, but you will not be joining us." She took Radeeka's face in her hands and kissed her forehead, each cheek, chin, and nose. "My dear Radeeka, I love you so much! You are growing up so fast! Our housekeeper has gone to visit her sickly mother and Mrs. Hamadani is busy for a while tonight, but your father and I agreed, you are eight years old and old enough to stay alone until Mrs. Hamadani can be here. We will be home by 10:00. You should practice your multiplication tables and be sleeping by 9:00. If you have any problem at all, Mr. Hamadani is just down stairs, as always."

"Yes, mama," she said as Ruchi kissed her forehead.

That night, Raj and Ruchi hugged her good night and left for the event. "Remember, if you need anything, ring Mr. Hamadani at the front desk."

"Yes, papa," she said as Raj kissed her forehead.

From the window, Radeeka saw them pause before getting into the backseat of a black town car. Raj and Ruchi both leaned back to see Radeeka at the window and blew her kisses.

Feeling quite grown up, Radeeka finished her homework and fell asleep. While she slept, Mrs. Hamadani entered silently, checked on Radeeka and settled in a chair to read.

Hours later, sirens in the street woke Radeeka. She pushed the curtain aside to see out of the window by her bed. In the distance, buildings were flashing red and blue from reflected police lights. She couldn't see the street.

She found Mrs. Hamadani reading a book in the living room. The reading lamp cast yellow light around her dark blue *hijab*. "Did the sirens wake you, Radeeka?"

Radeeka rubbed her eyes, nodded and walked into her parents' bedroom, feeling too grown up to climb into Mrs. Hamadani's lap. She wrapped herself in a blanket on their bed and breathed the scent of them. Fear cramped her heart.

Mrs. Hamadani sat on the bed rubbing Radeeka's back, "Go back to sleep my sweet, your mama and papa will be home soon." She hummed a Kashmiri lullaby until she thought Radeeka had fallen asleep.

Mrs. Hamadani returned to reading and soon fell asleep herself, still sitting in the chair.

Radeeka did not sleep.

As the sun came up, Radeeka tip toed to her own room to use the toilet. She fastened a barrette with three daises to hold her ponytail, put on her favorite t-shirt with a yellow kitten on the front, blue jeans and white sandals with white daisies like the barrette.

Papa's voice reminded Radeeka, *Always carry coins in your pocket, my sweet.*

Still careful not to wake Mrs. Hamadani, who slumped in the chair with a book in her lap, Radeeka tiptoed back to her parents' bedroom to pocket the coins Raj had left on the bureau for her.

By the front door, she pressed her palms together, bowed to Ganesh then rubbed his trunk with both hands. Her mother's voice echoed, T*he elephant god has blessed our family with prosperity and love.* She lingered, reluctant to release Ganesh. She soundlessly closed the door behind her and entered the elevator. She expected to find Mr. Hamadani at his post in the lobby, but she heard two policemen talking with him. Their voices echoed off the marble floor and walls. She recognized one of them. Her father often talked with him at the market. His hair was white above his ears, and he had a scar on one cheek, which exposed his teeth in a sneering half-smile. Frightened by him, Radeeka hid behind the desk and listened.

"... We are thinking brakes of the bus malfunctioned. The doctor and his wife were both killed along with their driver. The bus driver was also killed and people on the bus were badly injured. It was a horrific scene," said the scar-faced officer.

"We have just now opened the street to traffic," said the other as they stepped into the elevator. "We're going to their flat now. I wish I was having better news for that poor little girl. We have no choice but to take her to the orphanage." The elevator doors closed before Mr. Hamadani could tell the policemen about Raj's plans for Radeeka.

The policemen rapped on the door, waking Mrs. Hamadani. The officer began telling the story and she shushed him. "The child is sleeping. My husband and I will tell her the news." She informed them that she and her husband had been appointed by Dr. Khawaja to look after the girl. "We have the necessary papers. She will stay here with us."

She closed the door, walked from room to room, and realized Radeeka had left the flat. She hurried to catch the elevator.

Mr. Hamadani found Radeeka behind the desk, her face as pale as tea with milk. "Radeeka, where is my wife?" he asked in a thin voice that stuck in his dry throat.

"Sleeping in the chair."

"Did you hear the policemen, before they entered the elevator?"

She nodded, her dark eyes staring at nothing.

He pulled her into his arms. "Radeeka, I am so sorry." He released his hug, "My wife and I will care for . . ."

Radeeka wasn't listening. She walked stoically through the front door with her fingers rolling coins deep in both pockets. She stared at the beach across the street and heard her father's laughter dissolve in the warm breeze. She smelled the *samosas* her mother made for picnics. Then, she turned and ran as fast as she could.

Mr. Hamadani stumbled around his desk, through the door, and disappeared before his wife and the policemen exited the elevator.

He tried to catch Radeeka but she was too fast, darting into traffic, and beyond. He called his wife from a pay phone then searched for Radeeka until well after dark.

chapter 3

THE STREET

All day Radeeka wandered among the throngs of people in the heart of Mumbai, avoiding policeman she thought would take her to the orphanage. She shivered at the thought of being imprisoned there. She remembered the overpowering stench of rot and feces, and the feeling of disrepair, worse than anything she had experienced until then.

After sunset, Radeeka huddled in the doorway of a sari shop, blankly watching traffic in the street. She noticed a man on a red Vespa pause among the crush of traffic. His daughter stood on the floor at his feet, peering over the handle bars, her arms curled around his forearms. His wife rode sidesaddle behind him, wearing a cobalt, rose and yellow sari, hugging her husband's waist with one arm and a bag of groceries with the other. The little family's laughter rose above the putt-putt of their scooter, and faded as traffic moved on. Radeeka brought her knees to her chin, hugged her legs, and eventually fell into fitful sleep.

She awoke at dawn, needing to relieve herself. The sky glowed with rosy light. She squatted behind a garbage bin in the alley next to the sari shop and tried to keep her jeans clean.

As the street filled with the sounds of commerce and petrol fumes mixed with the smell of masala and cumin, her stomach rumbled. She pulled a coin from her pocket to buy two stale rolls from a food *wallah*.

The crowd of shoppers and tourists surged around her as she avoided eye contact. She passed beggars of all ages on street corners and in front of the market. A deformed man awkwardly pulled himself along the sidewalk with a dirty palm. His arms and legs bent into shocking angles,like a crushed spider. With fingernails filled with grime, he tapped his toothless mouth, "*bab-la, bab-la,*" while one elbow bent toward the sky. Tourists passed, looking straight ahead as if he were invisible.

In the median, between lanes of traffic, cows lazily swished their tails at incessant flies as traffic sped by. Standing among the cows, a woman held a blind baby with scars all over its body. "*Bab-la, bab-la*" she begged when traffic stopped. Occasionally a tourist would offer rupees but most drivers and passengers kept their eyes forward.

From a fountain in the round-about, with traffic rushing by, Radeeka lapped water with the cows. She bought fried dough from a food *wallah*. She longed to brush her teeth and wash her hands and face, imagining a shower, with hot water flowing through her hair.

Before dawn she doubled over with intestinal pain and spent most of the next three days behind a dumpster. High fever, vomiting, and diarrhea overwhelmed her. She shivered with chills even though the air temperature reached 110 F. When she slept, rats nibbled her ears and toes. Clammy and delirious, she screamed for her mama and papa. No one came to her aid.

When the fever subsided she was weak from dehydration, hunger, and lack of sleep, but she kept walking further from what had been her home.

She bought a roll but soon vomited on the curb.

A foreign shopper placed a bottle of water on a counter near Radeeka. She grabbed the bottle and melted into the crowd. She hid in an alley filled with garbage and took little sips of the warm water.

Street people of all ages did the needful wherever the need struck. Women lifted dirty saris to squat on the curb in full view of passersby. Men urinated on trees and buildings. Radeeka tried to hide behind trash bins and bushes as diarrhea became a daily reality. She was sore and itched from not cleaning herself. Her clothes reeked. In the wee hours, she crept into a fountain and tried to wash her t-shirt and soiled jeans. She ducked underwater to avoid being seen naked when a taxi passed by. She put on her wet, still-dirty clothes.

As days passed and her nausea subsided, she used her coins to buy bananas and rolls until she'd spent her last paise.

Her stomach growled and she pinched a banana when a fruit *wallah* turned away. She hid in the corner of an alley to savor the banana, including the skin.

In the market where tourists shopped, the foreign women carelessly put rupees into their pockets or left their handbags dangling open while they nervously bartered for trinkets. Radeeka waited for the right moment to nab their money.

One afternoon, as Radeeka slipped stolen rupees into

her pocket, someone grabbed her arm and roughly jerked her around. "Get lost! This is my territory!" said a boy about her size. His breath smelled of decay and garbage and stung her eyes.

Radeeka carefully scanned for clues to his situation and temperament. His eyes sunk into a dirty face. Bruises darkened his face and arms. Scabby wounds scored his head and legs. His clothes were the color of sandalwood bark, regardless of their original color. His trousers scarcely reached his dusty calves above callused and muddy bare feet. A blood-stained, blue shirt floated around him and hung mid-thigh. Black hair matted against his scalp. His words were harsh but behind his dark eyes she glimpsed shadows of kindness and fear.

Two weeks had passed since she ran from her home. Her clothes reeked, but the yellow kitten on her t-shirt was still visible. Each morning she combed her dusty hair with her fingers and put it back into a ponytail, but the three fabric daisies had fallen off of her barrette. Her fingernails were grimy and needed cutting. Her feet were dirty but her sandals still fit. Jamal failed to notice her full, healthy looking face and well-fitting shirt and pants.

"Maybe I could distract them while you lift money," she said to Jamal, hoping he would agree.

"Ever been caught?"

"No."

"Well I got caught lots a times, it's no fun."

"Did they take you to the orphanage?" she said with wide eyes and a shiver.

"No, you imbecile! I'm a thief, not an orphan. The police beat me until everything went black. I woke up in a cell full of angry murderers. I escaped when they loaded us for Author Road Prison."

I am an orphan and a thief, thought Radeeka, shivering again, in spite of the heat, "What's your good name?"

"They call me Jamal." He lifted his chest, and straightened his back as he spoke.

"How long have you been on the street, Jamal?"

His eyes narrowed, "What do you mean? How long? I'm here, that's all." The boy had experienced no other life. He rarely worried about the past or the future. He survived hour by hour, hand to mouth. In this lifetime, his fate was cast. He was ten years old but hadn't tallied the passing years. "I ran a gang of thieves for a while, but they scattered when I went to jail. I'll let you work my territory and see if you're worth it."

A few days later, Radeeka saw two children, around five or six years old, begging from the middle of an intersection. They jumped to avoid an accelerating taxi that swerved to hit them rather than avoid them.

She led the children to the sidewalk and introduced them to Jamal. The girl called herself Arana. Her little brother was mute because his tongue had been removed. Jamal liked having authority and allowed them to join his band of thieves if they followed his rules. He would sell the recyclables they gathered, as well as stolen items. He keep half for himself and shared the rest.

That night they all slept together under the fruit *wallah's* cart.

🐘 🐘 🐘

Twelve days after the accident, Dr. Keir Keefe attended a memorial service for Raj and Ruchi. The harsh musky scent of marigolds and pungent incense met him in the lobby of their building.

Mr. Hamadani and his wife wore white and sat next

to an easel with a meter tall portrait of Raj and Ruchi taken at the business celebration, an hour before they died. The frame was encircled with marigold garlands.

"Dr. Keefe, thank you for coming." Mr. Hamadani rose, and shook Keir's hand. "Allow me to introduce my wife."

"Pleased to meet you Mrs. Hamadani," said Keir as he bowed his head with respect. "I'm sorry it is under such circumstances."

Mrs. Hamadani placed her hands together, bowed her hijab-covered head. She remained seated while her husband talked to Keir.

"So sad," said Mr. Hamadani, "they had no living relatives except for their daughter."

"How is she handling the loss? They were wonderful parents, it must be dreadful."

"Radeeka has run away. I suspect she heard the policeman say he would be taking her to the orphanage. I am looking for her every day," said Mr. Hamadani. "I am hiring a doorman to take my place until I find her." He walked to his desk. "Here is a photo of Radeeka, with my phone number on the back. Please, if you see her, will you ring me at once?"

"Of course," said Keir

🐘 🐘 🐘

Radeeka awoke to find a tiny girl in a red party dress cuddled close to her chest.

Radeeka traced the red embroidery with her palm, aware of the fabric's fine quality. The child's cheeks were plump and she smelled of soap, flowers, and sweet milk. A small silver barrette held her hair away from her face. Radeeka peered into the girl's unusual golden eyes, "Your mother must love you very much. What is your good name?"

she said in Hindi.

The toddler didn't speak. She began her new life, looking into the eyes of each child, introducing herself without a sound.

"We will call you Shakti. My mother told me about the goddess of power. Shakti who is no one but part of everyone," said Radeeka.

Jamal didn't care about the child's unusual eyes, healthy glow, or expensive red dress. He snatched the silver barrette from her fine hair. "I can get a good price for this!" he crowed.

Radeeka grabbed his wrist and pried his grubby fingers open. "No! This barrette is all she has." Radeeka put it into her own pocket, where she once carried coins from her papa. "The barrette is not ours to sell."

Jamal grumbled but let her keep the barrette.

Radeeka hoisted the little one onto her hip and carried her wherever the pack roamed. Radeeka had known the love of a mama and papa; the other members of the pack did not.

Radeeka led the pack in meditation every morning and evening, "We must be grateful for every bite of food, for every kindness," she taught the others. "The more grateful we are, the more good things will come to each of us." The words were an echo of her father but she tried not to think of his closed eyes and pressed palms when they sat together in front of Ganeash every day.

Meditation helped Radeeka put her parents and her situation out of her mind and cope with her new reality but it also created a sense of belongingness among her packmates. Jamal thought the meditations were nonsense but sat with the others for the duration of Radeeka's chanting. Soon he wasn't as hungry or as afraid.

The smaller children stopped tourists in the market

with their big pitiful eyes, while Jamal and Radeeka pilfered money, cameras, watches, and other treasures. Jamal was experienced at selling such things. He called himself their leader, but it was Radeeka's governance that made them a family.

The pack of orphans survived on garbage or what little food they could buy. Shakti's tiny fingers scratched in garbage bins like a monkey grooming its sibling. Radeeka shared what she found.

Soon, Shakti couldn't remember the love of her mother, the security of her bed, the satiety of a meal, or her birth name.

🐘 🐘 🐘

Radeeka's jeans became too big around her waist. She found a string to cinch them above her hollow hips. Daily exposure to the harsh sun burned her soft face. She tried to finger comb her hair, but soon her fingers could not penetrate the tangles. Her barrette broke and her hair stood sun bleached and matted, in harmony with the chaos of her life. The yellow kitten on her shirt disappeared and the denim blue of her jeans vanished, as if she lived in a sepia photo. She no longer resembled the healthy, happy child from Chowpatty Beach.

chapter 4

CLAIRE—1995

*C*laire gathered her luggage from the carousel onto a trolley and stood in queue to clear customers with people of every nationality imaginable; from Africa to Switzerland, from England to China, from Argentina to Russia and beyond. Her blue silk pants suit looked fresh in spite of 21 hours of travel. In the waiting area beyond customs, among the sea of faces waiting for travelers, she saw a sign MRS. CLAIRE KAINE, held high by a gaunt and perspiring man dressed in a white shirt and black trousers. She pushed her trolley through the crowd, "Hello, I'm Claire Kaine."

He took control of her luggage saying, "Please come, I will be driving to Palace Hotel."

The hotel's car was a new white Ambassador designed like a 1952 Pontiac with spacious interior, large rounded fenders, and prominent sun visor. Most of the taxis lined up at the airport arrivals gate were white Ambassadors. The new-car smell mixed with a strong scent of curry and garlic.

The headlight's yellow glow came alive with dust as they left the parking area. Men on bicycles twisted in and out of the beams. She often traveled internationally and thought she had seen poverty, but nothing in her experience compared to the drive through Mumbai to the hotel. They passed hundreds of people sleeping on the sidewalk while millions more lived in huts made of cardboard, reed mats, and scraps of corrugated metal.

Under a streetlight a distraught woman with a chalky-tea complexion and eyes hidden in the shadows of her skulk, held a limp toddler draped over her bony arms. The child's head flopped back, its eyes and mouth open below swarming flies that glittered like fairy dust in the lamp light. The eyes were eerily lined with black *kohl* powder and the lifeless arms and legs dangled like socks filled with sand.

The plight of the mother and baby made Claire gasp for breath but she immediately controlled herself, not allowing the plight of others or the memory of her own grief to overtake her. The face she revealed to the world was always unruffled and strong. Her business life was her only life.

She checked into a Western-style room at the Palace Hotel. Isolated from the rest of India she could have been in a Chicago hotel. As always, she was too keyed up to fall asleep. She unpacked her bags and put her state-of-the-art laptop on the small desk. It was an IBM ThinkPad 365 with Windows 95, a 32 bit operating system, sound card and a CD player. As she unpacked, she listened to a recording of Varvara Ivanova, playing Handel's Harp Concerto with the Kremlin Chamber Orchestra.

She took a long hot shower, and slept soundly until noon.

Before going to the restaurant for lunch, she opened the heavy light-blocking curtains and stood by the window looking down into the hotel swimming pool. A slim European man sunbathed in a red speedo while two young

Muslim women splashed in their berkas. In the shadows, beyond the wall, cardboard shelters grew like mushrooms. Men squatted in a vacant lot klatching with their neighbors, and she realized they were communally answering the call of nature.

At lunch, the grilled tofu tasted like chicken. A side order of rice and dal arrived without request. The guidebook she'd read on the plane warned against unpeeled fruit or vegetables or any raw food, so she avoided the most beautiful red strawberries she had ever seen.

Waves of reflected light flickering above her on the restaurant ceiling were produced by infinity-edged pools spilling one into the next. Exotic white angel trumpet, yellow cassia, bird of paradise, and other tropical plants bordered the lush green grass and the tall brick wall that defined the hotel compound. Once inside, a guest of the Palace Hotel could imagine being in Hawaii or Dubai.

At 9:00 the next morning, as planned, Claire took a hotel taxi to the office. Wearing a light cotton summer suit, with a calf-length skirt and long sleeved jacket, she slid into the taxi and gave the driver a business card with the address.

He stopped in front of an unfinished shell of a concrete building not far from the hotel. "This can't be right! Are you sure this is the address?"

"Yes ma'am. This is being the office of Mumbai's new telephone company."

She entered through the double glass doors at street level, the only floor of the building that had glass in the windows. "You must be Mrs. Kaine. Welcome to Mumbai," said a man stepping from the shadows. He wore a handsomely tailored ecru western-style business suit. The light fabric contrasted with his smooth dark complexion and stylish long hair. He shook her hand vigorously, "I am Jaydeep Pradant, CEO of the local partner. We spoke on the phone."

"Hello, Mr. Pradant, so nice to meet you in person."

"This way, I'll show you to your office."

They walked through a large room with at least two dozen folding tables, some with folding chairs, scattered in no particular order.

He opened a large, western-looking office door, with a long narrow window on one side. They were met by a blast of cool air. "Allow me to introduce your administrative assistant, Janus. Don't hesitate to ask her for help adjusting to life in India as well as business matters."

"Hello Janus, nice to meet you." Claire reached to shake her hand.

"It is being my pleasure, Mrs. Kaine."

"Please, before we go further, I'd like to make something clear to both of you. I am not married, and please, call me Claire."

"Yes, ma'am, and please address me as Jaydeep."

"Yes, Miss Claire," said Janus.

Claire's office and the adjoining conference room were well appointed considering the chaos of the building's exterior and the rest of the first floor. The large wooden desk and conference table were exquisitely finished and the black leather office chairs were large and comfortable. An empty custom-made book case covered most of one wall of her office and the conference room wall held a large white-board, all lit by huge windows facing a small courtyard full of tropical plants.

"The head engineer and the marketing director arrive tomorrow. Are there offices for them as well?" For the first few weeks she would have a staff of two. Tom, the chief engineer was flying in from Pittsburgh. This was his fourth international assignment. He knew what he was getting into, to a point, although none of the team, including Claire, were prepared for the scope of the project in a place like Mumbai. Craig, the marketing director from Kansas City, was African American. He kept his hair and beard trimmed short and looked like an American movie star. He'd been part of the Hong Kong implementation team.

Another expat, Julie, would be joining them to help with customer service training once they were closer to launch. Claire had met Julie in Boston. Julie was nearly six feet tall, with honey-colored skin and a thick cap of blonde hair. Her musical accent defied identification, with its round English vowels and square African consonants. Her mother was Dutch and her father Indian. She had grown up in Tunisia, England and India, making her a valuable asset to the team.

"There are tables and chairs they can use," indicating the space they had walked through moments before. "We assumed you would want sales and customer service on the main floor, and engineering on the second floor near the switch, however, you can decide where you want each department. Once the building is finished, your office will be on the top floor of course."

Craig and Tom can share the conference room until their offices are ready, she thought.

"What is the construction time-line?" she asked, aware that their original eighteen-month plan was far too aggressive.

"Let's take a tour of the rest of the building and I'll explain as we go." Returning to the hot dusty environment of the construction site, he led her up the open concrete stairs on the outside of the building.

"A family was hired to do the tenant improvements. They will have the windows installed and the telephony switch-room enclosed before monsoon starts the first week of June."

"Does monsoon always start the first week of June?"

"Yes, this year the rain will begin on June seventh."

"I'll mark it on my calendar," she said, not meaning to sound sarcastic. He didn't notice.

The construction family lived on-site and managed domestic activities along with the work day. The women did laundry, cooked, tended the children, swept, and worked on the construction site carrying bricks to the brick layers. The only functioning toilet was the one in the executive office suite, which even Janus didn't use. She wanted to ask Jaydeep what facilities the workers used but decided against it. She didn't want to know.

"Every family member has a job, including the children. They work all day and sleep against the building in tents," he said.

A parade of eight dark-skinned extremely thin women, each balancing a board loaded with six oversized red bricks on her head, climbed past them toward the fourth floor. Some had toddlers on a hip or an infant in a sling on her back. The women were so thin Claire worried that their legs might buckle under the weight.

"It appears that these women are dressed differently than the women I've seen on the street or in the hotel. Are they wearing pants?"

"You are very observant, Miss Kaine. Most women in Mumbai wrap the Maharashtra style sari. These Shudra women are wearing *kasta*-style saris, with nine meters instead of five meters of fabric. They tuck the fabric at the waist to look, and function, like pants."

Women, not men, tended the children but the little

children took care of the even littler ones and the older children had assignments on the construction site.

"Members of the family also build the furniture, on site" he said.

Using ancient saws and broken hammers, Claire noticed. The table saw, the only power tool, was operated by a nine-fingered twelve-year-old boy. It had no plug so he pushed bare wire tips into an outlet and wedged a little stick to hold the wires in place. Throughout the project, Claire never saw a tape measure, ruler, level or any kind of measuring device, except when Sven and his team of engineers arrived from Stockholm to install the switch. Sometimes the finished product reflected local methods, but to her astonishment, her desk and the conference table were perfect.

One day Claire heard the foreman reprimand a four-or five-year-old girl. Her job was to collect recyclable ceiling material into a big white bag. Claire couldn't understand the Marathi but she did understand the tone. The little girl stood with her head bowed and didn't speak, apparently this was not a new experience for her.

Claire mentioned her concerns about on-site child labor practices to Janus.

"But Miss Claire, the children will be having a rupee for rice."

The monsoon began on June seventh as Jaydeep predicted but the second floor wasn't ready for the switch installation. As long as the family worked, they had a place to live, and no incentive to finish. When Claire realized this, she offered extra bonuses, and additional work on future projects if they finished the second floor before September. Progress improved.

chapter 5

LIFE IN INDIA

Tom and Craig persuaded Claire to join them for dinner at Tomatoes, an "American" restaurant recommended by a local engineer. They had eaten local cuisine since arriving in Mumbai and were looking forward to more familiar fare. American-looking Coca-Cola and Mobile Gas signs and other 1950s memorabilia decorated the walls. The menu looked deliciously familiar, as if they'd stepped into Billy McHale's Bar and Grill in Seattle.

Mouths watering, the men ordered Chicken Ranchero. Claire ordered Chicken Tenders. Their enthusiasm faded when the unpleasant waiter delivered three identical plates of rice, lentils, and tofu. Hands in her lap, Claire looked up from her plate, "Maybe the cook heard a rooster crow while he cooked?" she said.

Tom and Craig laughed and agreed.

"American decor but not American cuisine," said Craig.

"Glad I didn't convince my wife to join us," said Tom. "She'll be going back to Pittsburgh next week. She's not as adventurous as she thought she was."

"My wife'll be on the same plane outta here," said Craig. "Too bad. This city is so rich in culture and history; it's fascinating. On the trip over, she talked about volunteering, but facing the reality of the street children's lives really got to her. Yesterday she gave one little girl a rupee and others swarmed around her with their dirty hands out, begging and shouting. The driver brought her back to the hotel, and she hasn't left since."

"I understand why they want to go home," said Claire. "I traveled the world with my parents when I was a kid, I've seen a lot, but I'm not sure I could stay in Mumbai for a year if I wasn't working all day. The heat, the dirt, the smell. . . and the copious poverty. . . ."

"If every kid in America had to spend a month here, and I don't mean at the Palace Hotel, imagine how their attitudes would change. The contrast between affluence and poverty. . . I have trouble justifying my own life's choices when I watch those little kids eat garbage from trash bins," said Tom. "Last week at the market, I threw a banana peel into a trash bin and six little urchins dove for it. They pulled it apart and devoured it like candy."

After dinner, they returned to the hot, dark sidewalk where a dust-covered boy waited with his pet monkey, "*Bab-la, bab-la*" he begged, tapping his lips and startling white baby teeth. The monkey sported a hoop earring and humped the boy's head with affection. Tom gave the boy a rupee and soon a group of children followed him like the pied piper. "Hello sir, hello sir," they shouted, the only English words they knew. He gave them each a rupee.

A few meters from the car, where the driver had waited during dinner, a bent and wrinkled man in a bright orange turban begged with a dented tin cup while leaning heavily on a stick. His toothless jaw protruded in a disturbing angle, nearly swallowing his nose. Shadowy sockets hid his foggy, cataract-chocked eyes deep in his fleshless skull. A pattern of parallel old scars, probably caused by a bamboo reed, decorated his hunched back above a stained lungi. His mud-caked bare feet were bony, callused, and cracked. As the three Americans slid into the waiting car, Craig put a 100 rupee note, about $3US, into the man's cup. Inside, as the car pulled from the curb, Craig said, "Maybe putting money in his cup encourages begging and isn't the best way to help, but I'm pretty sure that old guy won't buy liquor with it." He wiped his eye with his sleeve.

Claire had a similar reaction. Stepping into the shocking poverty after a warm meal in the generally American atmosphere of Tomatoes, Claire's eyes burned from the strain of avoiding tears in front of Tom and Craig.

On the way back, Tom wanted to stop at a drug store to buy a bottle of aspirin.

The driver was confused.

"Pharmacy?" said Tom.

Still the driver looked puzzled.

Tom looked at Claire, "any ideas?"

"Chemist?" she suggested.

"Achha, Achha. Chemist, I drive to Chemist, it is not too much very far. Chello."

The driver stopped in front of small cabin-like building on cinder block stilts. Tom walked up the three rough cement steps. The chemist, wearing a once-white shirt, dusty black trousers and bare feet, sat on a stool clipping his toe nails. Shelves around him were stocked with first aid supplies and medications of all sorts. Tom asked for aspirin.

"How many will you be wanting sir?" said the Chemist, with his head bobbing side to side.

"Just one, please," said Tom. Without washing his hands, the Chemist opened a small sachet and spilled one tablet into his palm. Tom changed his order to six packets and was charged one hundred rupees for each packet, about $1.50 US per aspirin.

Every Friday, the company attorney came to the office to deliver the per diem to Claire and her team. Each expat, including the wives, received a brown paper bag stuffed with a huge stack of rupees. Each brown bag held more money than many Indian families made in a lifetime.

During the first few weeks in India, the women frequented the hotel shops, spending their rupees on rugs they would never put on a floor, colorful silk saris they would never wear, handmade pottery and brass cooking utensils they would never use, all priced at 100 times the local rate. They were reluctant to expose themselves to the angry beehive of humanity where the smell of human waste, acrid cooking fires, and sweet flowers combined with the crush of people, cows, dusty air, and overwhelming heat, making the shortest walk quite unpleasant.

Tom and Craig hired an air-conditioned car to give them a tour of the city. The driver parked at Mumbai's Colaba Causeway market and opened the car door, "here we shop now." He guided them to shops where they could barter for tinkling glass bracelets they would never wear and brass singing bowls they would never understand. He accepted his cut from each merchant after every purchase.

The women took pity on the dirty street children and gave them rupees. During the confusion, they never noticed that the colorful rupees, that looked to them like play money, had been lifted from their pockets.

Indian currency could not be converted to US dollars so every rupee went toward supporting the local economy, either through a merchant or a pick-pocket.

Claire had no time for shopping. Most of her food was charged to her room and paid for by her employer. She opened a savings account at the Bank of Maharashtra to deposit her per diem. Meanwhile, the company deposited 100% of her salary in her Seattle bank account.

🐘 🐘 🐘

While Claire ate her lunch at the hotel a group of homeless children began to play in the fountain near the entrance.

Appalled by the filthy children, Claire called the waiter to her table to complain. "Can't you do something about those dreadful . . ." But when she saw the tiny girl taking off her red dress and placing it by the tree, she waved the waiter away. "Never mind." The children weren't just playing, they were bathing and drinking the water.

Claire's heart began to ache but she refused to allow the emotion. She turned her back, and focused on a report she brought along to read during lunch.

Absentmindedly, she asked the waiter to put her leftovers in a container. As she left the comfort of the excessively air-conditioned hotel, the angry heat took her breath. She regarded the white plastic bag holding a Styrofoam container, *What am I thinking? I'll never eat this.*

Most days, she took a hotel taxi a few blocks to the office but inexplicably, on this smoldering, pre-monsoon afternoon, she decided to walk. She paused by the fountain where the squealing children splashed each other. The water sparkled like sequins in the sunlight and glittered on their wet brown skin.

Claire couldn't help thinking that the little girl was

about the age of her own daughter, lost so long ago. She shook her head, dashing the thought.

From the corner of her eye Claire saw the hotel manager walking through the boiling, humid air toward the fountain. With two fingers, she picked up the dirty red dress and offered it to the girl as she climbed out of the fountain.

Their eyes locked, Claire's as aquamarine as the Mediterranean Sea, the little girl's, as golden as a leopard's gaze. Momentarily overcome by the intensity of the energy between them, Claire almost dropped the Styrofoam box before offering it to the child.

The girl's chin lifted as she breathed in the aroma of warm, fresh food. She pulled the dress over her head, timidly accepted the food with both hands and a nod, and ran beyond the wall with the others.

On Sunday Claire left the hotel after lunch with a Styrofoam container in a white plastic bag just as the little girl appeared at the fountain without the other children.

Sitting on a bench in the shade of a mimosa tree Claire patted the place next to her, "Sit," she smiled. "How old are you, sweetie?" *She doesn't speak English, of course,* thought Claire. Claire patted the bench again.

The girl climbed up.

Claire washed the child's hands and face with Handi-Wipes from her purse before offering the box of food and plastic fork. Fascinated by the activity, the girl sniffed the air. Ignoring the unfamiliar fork, she scooped with her fingers. She devoured the leftover rice and dahl, looking up with darting eyes like a starving dog after each bite.

When she'd finished the last grain of rice, Claire gently washed the child's hands and face again.

"My name is Claire," she said, patting herself, "Claire, Claire." She touched the girl's shoulder, "What's your name?"

The girl's eyes began to twinkle with recognition.

"Shakti," she said with a tiny voice as her hand touched her own chest.

The hotel manager abruptly appeared, "Is that dirty beggar child giving you a bother madam?"

Shakti jumped off the bench but winced as he gripped her shoulder.

"Let go of her at once. She is with me."

"Madam, it is being a bad idea to be feeding beggar children. Soon she will be having the others joining her," said the hotel manager as his head wagged from side to side, faster than usual.

"I see no other children here. Leave us." Claire's voice commanded compliance. The hotel manager offered a small bow and retreated to the lobby.

Shakti's big eyes grew wider. She didn't understand the English words Claire spoke to the man, but she sensed the woman's power. "Namaste" she nodded and disappeared into the crush of humanity beyond the wall.

Shakti came to the fountain several times each week, sometimes alone. She ate lunch with Claire on the bench, then escaped into the alley carrying a white plastic bag filled with extra meals and bottled water for the others.

chapter 6

SHAKTI—2016

I remember nothing of life in my father's house. In my dreams however, my mother carries me in the garden. I cling to her long black braid, and toy with the barrette at the end. I smell the passion flowers. I take my first steps in warm green grass.

Now I understand my mother's choice to leave me on the street rather than at the orphanage, which, I have no doubt, my father demanded. I learned from experience, the orphanage was a dreadful place where dreams melted into despair.

For over a year, I lived with a group of street children, like a feral family. At first I missed my mother and wondered why she left me. I couldn't communicate because I didn't understand Hindi spoken by the others. I couldn't even tell them my name. I can never know for certain but I suspect my mother spoke to me in Punjabi, a dialect from the north where she was born.

Radeeka was old and wise at eight years old. I felt safe with her. She named me after a goddess her mother had worshiped. I didn't learn my birth name until twenty-two years later. How do I thank Radeeka? Not just for taking care of me, but also for saving the barrette I wore in my hair that day, the single clue to my identity.

Life on the street meant never bathing, drinking from puddles, and eating garbage, sometimes bugs, and always watching for danger. One morning, a taxi pulled up to the curb next to us. The driver cast an evil light. I yelled "RUN!" but a man jumped from the back seat, grabbed Arana and her little brother then jumped back into the taxi and sped away before any of us could move. Radeeka, Jamal and I huddled together, too startled to run. Of course, we never knew what happened to Arana and her brother.

🐘 🐘 🐘

As we splashed and laughed in the hotel fountain one afternoon, Radeeka yelled "Run, hurry!" as the hotel manager walked toward us. I dashed toward the dress I'd left by the palm tree. A blond woman handed it to me along with a box of rice and dahl that smelled so good. For just an instant, I couldn't breathe. I had never seen eyes so blue, or skin so pale but I felt I had known her before I was born. Bright light glowed between us and I had no doubt she would be important in my life.

chapter 7

MEETING KEIR—1995

As Claire sat beneath the mimosa tree, hoping Shakti would join her, a man appeared by the bench. Tall and slender, he had a narrow nose that matched his frame, and kind green eyes with flecks of hazel. His demeanor was as comforting and none-threatening as a calm sea and his smile was enchanting and bright despite his crooked teeth, "Good afternoon," he said in an English accent, doffing his Panama hat. "Are you waiting for the little girl?"

Claire's face snapped toward him. "How do you know about the girl?"

"Allow me to introduce myself. I am Dr. Keir Keefe…. Do you mind if I sit down?"

Claire gave him her business smile and nodded toward the other end of the bench.

"I've watched her," he said, squinting through the glare toward the fountain. "At first an older girl carried the child on her hip, but the little one has grown…." he shook his head, ran his fingers through a thick tuft of red curls, and sighed. "I saw you giving her food. I'm certain of your good intentions, but I'm sorry to say this ma'am, you might not be helping her as much as you think you are."

Claire's back stiffened. "She can't be more than three years old and she's malnourished. What am I to do, watch her eat garbage, if any-thing at all?"

Keir heard more than outrage in Clair's voice. He felt her soft and vulnerable inner core, hidden behind her business facade. "What will happen when you leave?" his voice kind and concerned. "She won't know how to fend for herself."

Claire took a deep breath, and kept her chin high. "I can't bear to think of leaving her. An occasional lunch with her is the highlight of each week in this godforsaken place." Her eyes scanned the mass of humanity teeming beyond the hotel entrance, a cacophony of horns blaring in the intense dusty heat, buses, taxis, scooters, trucks, auto rickshaws, and men shouting behind ox carts. Reedy women, covered in colorful flowing saris, balanced baskets of food or laundry on their heads and toddlers on their hips. "I'm thinking of taking her home with me, so she'll have a chance at a better life."

"How long do you plan to stay in India?"

"Wish I knew," she said. "We're building a telecom network. We planned to have it up in eighteen months but now that we're here, it's obvious progress will be quite slow."

He rose, casting a small mid-day shadow as he stepped into the glaring sunshine, "I see the child just there." He bent his head toward the wall. "I'll leave you to get on." Shading his eyes with his hat he said, "Will you have dinner with me tonight? Perhaps we can discuss the fate of street children in India."

Claire nodded and surprised herself by saying, "That would be nice."

"Give us a bell when you return. I'm in room 222," he said. He put on his hat and climbed into the backseat of a waiting Mercedes.

Her eyes followed the car into traffic.

🐘 🐘 🐘

Around 6:30 pm, Claire returned to her room and dialed 222. "Hello, Keir, this is Claire."

"Ah, thanks for phoning. As we drove away, I realized I failed to ask your name. Claire. A lovely moniker for a lovely lady. I know a splendid restaurant where we can eat an authentic Indian meal with no worries of contracting Deli-belly. It's called Bhojan Thali. Are you ready for a quiet dinner?"

"Do I have time for a quick shower? The electricity was off in our building this afternoon. It got up to 125 in there."

"No worries, let's meet in the lobby at half seven, if that allows enough time."

Claire arrived in the lobby ahead of Keir. She wore wide-legged pants, a loose-fitting cap sleeved blouse, with a long shawl draped over her shoulders, all in gauzy shades of cerulean that accentuated her eyes and flawless fair skin. The soft outfit draped around her like a breezy summer sky.

"Splendid, you're ready." Keir stepped from the elevator at precisely 7:30, "My driver will meet us in the portico."

When he placed his palm in the small of her back to guide her through the lobby, her breath caught in her throat. She tried to remember the last time she had felt the tingle of a man's touch.

Keir introduced Claire to his driver, Ashook, who bowed as Claire scooted into the car. Ashook was polite and accommodating, with a big grin and happy eyes.

"Nice to meet you, Ashook," she said, then to Keir, "Nice vehicle."

"Yes, Ashook keeps me safe and comfortable while moving around in this overcrowded city."

"Where are we going for dinner?"

"Bhojan Thali, it's about an hour's drive. How well do you know Mumbai?"

"Sadly, I've been here a month but haven't left the hotel except for the office. This is an adventure for me," she said.

"Can I make something clear? Please?" he said in a pleading tone. "This is a date. I haven't been on a date in years. I'm a little nervous."

"I'm in the same boat," she sighed. "My career leaves little time for a personal life. I think that's one reason why little Shakti is having such an impact on me."

"Is that her name? Shakti?"

"Yes, she's an incredibly bright little girl," Claire said.

"Tell me, have you ever been married?" said Keir.

She looked at him. "I thought we were talking about Shakti."

He smiled, "I thought we were talking about being on a date."

"Oh, yes, well, sorry. No, engaged in college but—never married," she answered, squirming in her seat, fluffing her bangs, fidgeting with the armrest.

"You never longed for the fairy tale and the white picket fence?" he said.

"My parents were professors, Dad archaeology, Mom anthropology—very intellectual—they were both over forty when I was born. My nanny and I accompanied them on archaeological digs when I was as young as Shakti."

As they talked, Ashook drove them through the business district. Men wore dark suits and ties, as if in

Manhattan. The women wore colorful saris or *salwar* outfits with their *dupattes* flowing behind them as they moved with confidence.

On Claire's first traverse of Mumbai, after her flight landed, the sun had set leaving the streets shadowy and remote. This time, the abusive sunlight waxed the city with harsh reality. As Ashook drove beyond the business district a diffident world revealed itself.

Deformed, dull-eyed children begged from the median near stoplights as the car passed miles of cardboard ghetto. One young female panhandler was painted blue like Kali the Hindu Goddess of darkness. Her tongue protruded from her mouth, held in place by a rough wooden peg. Claire turned away, but the image was burned in her brain like a commercial jingle, repeating, unbidden.

Next to the curb, a colorfully dressed woman bathed a screaming naked toddler in a metal pot filled with muddy water. Men squatted in doorways built with sticks and discarded cement sacks.

Claire forced her focus back inside the car. "When I was young I dreamed of sailing the world, taking pictures and writing stories for the newspaper," she said. "I never played house like most little girls. Most of the time I was the only child among the adults. When I got older I couldn't imagine a life small enough to put a fence around. Here I am, CEO, bringing high-tech communications to a third world country." She took deep breath. "How about you, married, children?"

"I planned to have a big family and live in a 300 year old cottage near Bath, but Jennifer, my wife, died in a car accident just after our first wedding anniversary. We were twenty-two. We hardly had time to get to know each other. For ten years, I numbed myself with self-medication and alcohol while I finished med school," he laughed nervously. "Don't be alarmed, I've been clean and sober for over eleven years."

"How awful. Losing a loved one so young . . . is difficult. . . ." She had experienced the pain of losing a loved one. She avoided the memory of her daughter who had died at just three years old. To distract herself, Claire did the math in her head: *he was married at twenty-two, one year together, ten years of drugs and eleven years sober, that makes him a few years younger than me.*

As the sky turned the color of over-ripe plums, Ashook pulled up to a gated estate known as Bhojan Thali. A guard wearing a crisp white shirt and pressed black trousers greeted Ashook with a handshake and opened the gate.

The estate was a tropical version of New York City's Central Park in the middle of Mumbai. Shadowy mango trees filled with ripe yellow fruit lined one side of the driveway, the fragrant flowers of Indian Beech trees glowed like phosphorescent celestial nebulae gathered near the earth. Clusters of watermelon-sized prickly fruit grew from the trunks and limbs of jackfruit trees. A group of gnarled trunks with flamboyant red flowers and fern-like leaves welcomed them with open arms. Flocks of bright green parrots clung like leaves and took flight joining other exotic birds, flapping wings, singing songs and floating on warm air above the exotic flowers.

Keir rolled down the car window, "The air smells sweeter and sweeter as we get further from the multitudes. India must have been truly splendid before human-kind overpopulated this land."

"I didn't realize I'd become so accustomed to the sour air." She took a deep breath. "Lovely."

"We'll be eating outdoors," he told her as the car passed

white-washed buildings. "This restaurant serves traditional southern food. We'll eat with our fingers, right hand only, no silverware, while seated on cushions on the ground." He reported like a nervous tour guide. "I assume you haven't done this sort of thing before."

"No, this is new for me." When she saw patrons seated on the ground she whispered, "Glad I wore pants."

"Ah, yes, well, I didn't think of that. . . You look scrumptious by the way."

The waiter led them to their table and again Keir put his palm in the small of her back. She liked the feel of it, reassuring, not overpowering.

The table, set with banana leaves and glowing candles, stood just over a foot high. They sat with their legs crossed. Their knees touched and she sensed a sparkle between them.

"How did you find this place?"

"Lovely, isn't it? Ashook's recommendation. It's owned by his uncle and auntie. They serve a vegetarian menu, the best authentic southern Indian food you'll find in Mumbai, maybe the world."

"I love culinary adventures, but I've been reluctant. Delhi Belly is a reality I try to avoid," she said.

"No worries. The kitchen is immaculate. On my first visit, Ashook took me on a tour in broad daylight. The cooks are marvelous. All of them speak English and understand Western sanitation standards. The head chef attended culinary school in San Francisco. Nothing is served raw except for the fruit grown here on their property. You can eat any dish the waiters bring round."

The tall young waiters wore white *pajama kurtas*, white gloves, and marigold-colored turbans. One of them offered a basket filled with steaming finger-tip towels. Keir kept his left hand under the table and manipulated the towel with his right. Claire tried to follow suit, as the scent of lime filled the air.

Soft and pliable naan, brushed with ghee, was offered hot from the tandoori oven. It smelled and tasted like magic, nothing like the flat dry dough served at the hotel. They helped each other tear the naan into manageable pieces. One server spooned a few small mounds of white rice onto the banana leaves in front of each of them. Other servers moved among the low tables, spooning spicy, sweet, or pungent sauces onto the white rice. Claire eagerly tried them all, scooping the bright green, deep red, and dazzling yellow sauces with pieces of naan while unfamiliar exotic fragrances wafted around them.

Several times, Claire's left hand crept out from under the table but she jerked it back. "It's so difficult to keep my left hand on my lap while maneuvering my right," she whispered. "I never dreamed I could eat rice with my fingers!"

After dinner, they were ushered toward another tall bearded man in a marigold turban. He held a pitcher of warm jasmine water, with a clean white towel draped over his arm. Keir bent and offered his right hand.

"I'm so glad you were first," Claire whispered. "I would have offered both hands."

"That's what I did on my first visit. The poor man was horrified. I retracted my left hand, but the damage was done."

As they waited for the car, Claire said, "Oh, wait, we didn't pay for the meal," and turned to go back.

He touched her shoulder, "No worries, they'll bill me at the hotel."

"The meal was wonderful. Thank you. I'm so full. . . I wonder if Shakti had anything to eat tonight."

"Remember, the life she has is the only life she knows. You shouldn't feel guilty. She is a remarkable little girl. She will find her way in the world, with or without our help."

She turned to face him, "How do you know she's remarkable?" Claire said in a slightly confrontational tone.

"I've watched her from my hotel room and in the market." Someday he would explain the intelligent turquoise aura surrounding the child, but he thought Claire would think him peculiar if he mentioned it now. "She was so tiny. One day I followed them. I wanted to see where the poor little thing slept at night. It was deplorable." He looked away and closed his eyes. "When it got dark, she cuddled next to the older girl, and a boy, like puppies on the sidewalk next to a street light. She has less than nothing. Even if she had a comb, or a change of clothes, she would have no place to put them. The sad truth of it is, she's just one of millions of girl babies abandoned on the streets of India every year. I can't imagine. . . I don't want to imagine. . . what dreadful things happen to them."

Claire looked out the window, fighting her emotions, "I'm not leaving India without her," she promised.

Keir put his arm around her shoulders and she leaned into the comfort. For just a little while, she gave herself permission to feel like a woman, instead of a corporate executive. They rode the rest of the way in silence.

"Shall we have a spot of brandy in the bar?" he suggested as they got out of the car.

"I'd like that."

As if stepping into the The Alexis in Seattle, they walked among westerners eating and drinking in dim light. They settled at a small table with a vase of tropical flowers and a candle. The bartender, dressed in a white shirt, black trousers, and long burgundy Nehru vest, served brandy snifters balanced on tumblers filled with hot water. They rolled the warm snifters in their palms. Her heart beat a bit faster as she watched Keir mindfully enjoy the warm brandy in his mouth and throat.

"Living in India, particularly at the Palace Hotel, is like living in some sort of surreal time warp."

Claire agreed. "My employer arranged for me to live in a furnished flat. I hope it will help me feel more at home. I'm moving next week."

"Ah, you don't feel safe in the same hotel with me?" he hung his head, feigning despair.

She laughed. "I've been here a month! How long have you been here?"

"Over three years now."

"Really? You've lived in a hotel room for three years?"

"I have a long-term suite on the second floor. . . arranged by the university where I work. I'm on a five year assignment. Tell me, what are your plans for Shakti?"

"I'm not sure. My flat has two bedrooms and local-style maid's quarters. The complex was built for expats. If I hire a live-in nanny, Shakti could live with me. . . and maybe go to school. . ."

"And when your assignment is over? Then what?"

"I don't know. . . somehow. . . I'll take her with me." She took a sip of brandy. Determined not to show her emotions, she changed the subject, "Do you know where I could find a yoga class?"

He understood her need to talk of other things. "I might. I belong to a health club not far from here." He paused, "I've never seen a woman there, however. Certainly you can find a yoga class in Mumbai! There might be a class here in the hotel, I'd suggest asking the manager."

"Great idea, thank you," she sighed. "I think I'll go to

my room now. I have a busy day tomorrow." She reached for her purse and noticed her yellow fingertips, "Why are my fingers yellow? I washed my hands!"

"They're stained from the turmeric in the sauces," he said, curling his fist to look at his own fingers. Ask room service to send up some lime wedges."

"Ah, yes, good idea." As she stood, she opened her purse, "My secretary had personal cards printed with my new address and phone number, mostly to give taxi drivers. Would you like one?"

"Yes-please-of-course, I hope to see you again," he said, accepting the card with both hands. "Thank you."

"Maybe you can stop by when I get settled. The flat is furnished but I still need a few things to make it home. . . ." Tears welled and clung to her fair lashes. She couldn't stop them.

"What is it?"

She shook her head as if she could shake away the sadness. "More and more, I think of the contrast between my good fortune and the street children of India. . . . That phrase just now. . . a few things to make it home. . . sounded so absurd." Her arms flopped to her sides in frustration. "My life seems meaningless and hollow in contrast. Sometimes the stress of living and working in this country is just too much." She covered her face with her hands, wiped her eyes, raised her chin, and straightened her back.

"There isn't an expat in-country who wouldn't agree with you. There's a reason why big corporations call this a hardship assignment. One thing I've noticed though, the street children seem happy. They don't perceive the scarcity. They expect nothing more. Their lives are filled with a different kind of abundance. They live for now, the present moment. We should be so wise."

chapter 8

REMEMBERING JENNIFER

Keir rubbed his fingers with a lime wedge to remove the turmeric stains then stepped into the shower. The steaming hot water ran through his hair and over his face but he kept his eyes closed and lips tightly sealed. Hotel management insisted that the tap water was safe but he'd been in India long enough to know it may or may not be safe on any given day . . . *Oh so sorry for inconveniencing you sir, the system, it has been having a leak in filtration.* Keir considered three days of stomach cramps and diarrhea more than mere inconvenience.

As the hot water washed over him, he thought of the children in the fountain. What if this shower was the first in his life? He wouldn't care that he must close his mouth or shut his eyes. The street children, especially the tiny three year old, reminded him to be grateful. He dried off with a cloud-like terry towel and crawled between clean white sheets, appreciating the fresh smell, the softness, the comfort.

Then, as he lay in the dark, listening to the discord of music, dancers' drums, and night noises of Mumbai, he thought of Jennifer.

*** *** ***

Keir and Jennifer met in an undergraduate chemistry class at the University of Bath. They were inseparable after their first date. They moved into a picturesque thatch-roofed cottage near Bath. Originally built in 1711 by Jennifer's ancestors, the cottage was bequeathed to Jennifer by her grandparents.

Keir and Jennifer drove back to Bath from a delayed honeymoon at the Grosvenor House Hotel across from Kensington Palace. It was their first anniversary. The hum of tires on wet pavement lulled Jennifer to sleep after a busy week in London. They'd spent days roaming museums, shopping at Harrods and having afternoon tea. Then they played in bed and took a nap before getting dressed to go out, one night Oh! Calcutta! his choice, and another night Chauviré and Nureyev at the Royal Ballet, her choice.

Damp pavement reflected the headlights. They were the only car on the road. She cuddled next to him as he drove with his left arm around her. *Life couldn't be better,* he'd thought.

Cresting a knoll, a lorry loaded with steel beams drifted into Keir's path. Both drivers swerved to miss a head-on crash. The lorry's brakes screeched as it jackknifed. Keir's Peugeot spun out of control and lodged under the lorry. Rescue teams worked for hours in heavy rain to free Keir and Jennifer from the wreckage. The impact threw Jennifer into the back seat. She had no obvious injuries. Internal injuries killed her instantly.

Rescuers were surprised to find Keir alive in the mangled wreckage. A forehead wound bled profusely. His legs were broken in several places, the steering column crushed his chest, and his right arm was broken. His damaged heart required defibrillation several times in the ambulance.

Recovering from his injuries had taken fourteen months in hospital, the first month in a drug-induced coma. It took another year of surgeries and intense physical therapy for him to walk again. His broken heart never fully healed. Once he'd beaten his addiction to pain medication, he drank beer to forget and gin to remember.

He recovered physically, but gave up his plan to establish a private practice. He accepted a position at the University of Bristol medical school and applied for a research grant to study ayurvedic medicine.

One day Nigel, his colleague and best friend, entered his classroom as the students filed past. Keir and Nigel played tennis every afternoon. Nigel was taller and thinner than Keir. His bald head gave him the stature of a pencil standing on its point.

Keir pulled a green crew-neck sweater over his head as they walked through the cool damp air past the Roman architecture of Victoria Rooms toward the Pulse Gym. Nigel said, "Did you see the posting for the position in Mumbai? You should consider it. Sounds like a brilliant opportunity to research your barmy obsession with ayurvedic medicine."

"India might be the perfect place to study ancient healing practices, but it would take an outrageous compensation package to persuade me to live in bloody India."

"Double the salary, a suite at a 5 star hotel, a full time driver, and only fifteen hours per week in the classroom." Nigel stopped and turned to look Keir in the eye. "Keir, my friend, you must leave England. It's as if Jennifer is following you everywhere."

A few days later, Keir received a letter from his sister. Adela and her husband, Norbert, lived in the United States while they both earned PhDs in Anthropology at Princeton. Adela wrote to let Keir know that Bert had been offered a position at the University of Bath. The next morning, Keir accepted the India assignment and offered the bungalow to his sister, rent free, for the duration of his assignment in India.

🐘 🐘 🐘

Keir landed in Mumbai at 5:30am. It was early June. Standing in the queue at customs, he choked on hot air filled with cigarette smoke and body odor. The flight attendant had announced that temperatures were cooler now, only 33 degrees C, because the monsoon had begun, but runnels of perspiration trickled down his back.

Just beyond customs, a young man held a clearly printed sign DR. KEIR KEEFE.

"I'm Doctor Keefe."

The handsome young man shook his hand. He was as tall as Keir, with straight black hair, and smooth, clear skin. A strong jaw anchored his big white smile. He had a robust, healthy looking physique, not gaunt like most of the drivers who waited for a fare, and his big eyes flashed with intelligence. "Hello, sir. My name is Ashook. I am your driver. My car is always ready to transport you as you wish."

Ashook took control of the trolley holding Keir's luggage and led him to the car through the humid air filled with the raucous horns and exhaust fumes. Mumbai couldn't have been further from Bath. The contrast was staggering. Exactly what Keir needed. Memories of Jennifer would no longer confront him at every turn.

The car's air conditioner strained to cool the interior of the immaculate Mercedes as Ashook drove through the muddy streets. They passed miles and miles of shacks made of wet cardboard and worn bamboo mats. The magnitude of poverty was beyond any Keir could imagine and he began to doubt his five-year commitment.

He had stepped back through a portal of time, leaving Jennifer's memory in the present.

🐘 🐘 🐘

At the University of Mumbai, after teaching graduate anatomy classes and one in basic surgery, Keir enjoyed afternoon tea with his fellow researchers while they discussed the Vedic texts, ayurveda medicine, and methods of energy healing. The professors seemed oblivious to the poverty surrounding them, as if karmic destiny had put them in the upper caste and they need not be bothered during this lifetime.

Keir could not ignore it.

After he'd settled into his suite at the hotel and met his students, Keir asked Ashook to be his tour guide. He began to explore Mumbai from the comfort of his personal air-conditioned car.

Then one Friday after work, he told Ashook to take the weekend off; he would not be needing him until Monday. With his Nikon single-reflex camera, and bag of lenses slung over his shoulder, Keir walked the streets for hours, snapping the bright colors and contrasting architecture. Tall brick walls protected whitewashed mansions. Monkeys groomed each other on the ledges of extravagant government buildings. He photographed women balancing huge baskets on their heads. They floated along the sidewalk, their feet hidden beneath radiantly colored saris. Women in a heavy black *burkas* peered through the embroidered mesh that covered their eyes. Men wore white *dhotis*, *pajama kurtas*, vibrantly colored turbans, or western business suits. Parents showered their children with love, regardless of their caste.

Keir used his telephoto lens to furtively capture images of beggar children and their dirty faces full of white smiles. He found them happy despite their indigent existence. He gave them rupees while guarding his pockets, regardless of how charming they seemed.

🐘 🐘 🐘

One day, as Ashook drove him back to the hotel after work, they passed a gray stone wall, imbued with misery and despair. "What is this place, Ashook? I can feel the sadness clear out here."

The strength of Keir's natural perception made Ashook smile. "It is a place to take babies."

"You mean an orphanage."

"In India, boy babies are desired, girl babies not so much. Also some fathers do not have rupees to care for handicapped children or to feed second born sons." said Ashook.

The next day, Keir asked Ashook to drive him to the orphanage. "Ashook, is there a donation basket that you know of?"

"Yes, it is in the back wall, that way. It is where they put the babies. Would you like me to make the deposit for you?"

"No Ashook, I must do this myself."

Keir walked around the wall, avoiding garbage. In the back alley, he pushed on a worn window-size opening. The metal hinges squeaked, exposing the tattered basket where babies were "donated." He left a brown paper bag filled with 4,000 rupees, about 100 British pounds.

So began his weekly donation.

🐘 🐘 🐘

The administrative assistant in the Dean's Office, Paku, visited the orphanage whenever she could. She read to the crippled old residents who were left there long ago by parents who lacked the resources to care for them. One afternoon, as she approached the stone wall, she saw Dr. Keefe put his brown paper bag into the basket, but he didn't see her.

Weeks later, the small woman entered Keir's empty classroom. Metal-framed glasses made her beautiful dark eyes look even bigger. "Hello, Dr. Keefe. My name is Paku. I am an administrative assistant in the Dean's office. We received a request to send a doctor to the orphanage. One of the nuns has become ill. Would you be able to visit her after class today?"

"Nice to meet you Paku." He shook her hand. "I'd be happy to."

🐘 🐘 🐘

Two Sisters glowed like celestial angels as their white sari's reflected the afternoon sun, but the creaking wooden door extinguished the sunlight in the murky, colorless interior.

"This way please Dr. Keefe. We will take you to Sister Dilu." He followed the nuns down a long, gloomy corridor. The walls echoed with the click of his heels. The Sisters stepped soundlessly in canvas slippers. The air had a musty odor that reminded Keir of wet dogs and sour dishcloths.

Sister Dilu rested in a sagging cot in a room filled with similar beds. He lowered himself onto a tiny stool beside her and circled her cold bony hand with his long warm fingers.

Translucent, parchment-like skin stretched over Sister Dilu's skeletal frame. Her raspy voice trembled with age. "Doctor Keefe, I must admit that I sent for you falsely. I am old, tired, and ready to go home. Before I go, I want to thank you. This orphanage is poor and your generosity has helped the people who must stay here." The old nun balanced herself on a brittle elbow as a coughing spell consumed her. She held a white cloth to her mouth to absorb the blood. Keir supported her back until she caught her breath and fell back onto the cot.

"Our residents occasionally need medical care," she rasped, wiping more blood from her colorless lips. "Would it be possible for you to check on them from time to time?"

"Yes, of course, but isn't there something I can do to make you more comfortable, Sister?"

"You have done more than you can ever know. I must rest now." With a slight wag of her head, she said, "Sister Tia will see that you have a tour of our facility." Translucent eyelids settled over her foggy eyes.

"Please. Come with me, doctor," said Sister Tia, standing behind him.

Keir never learned how the Sisters discovered his identity.

Sister Tia led Keir to a small dark room lined with cribs. Tiny newborns slept with their knees tucked under them. His eyes stung with the scent of ammonia and unchanged diapers as he made a mental note to bring diaper rash cream and a supply of cloth diapers on his next visit.

She led him into a larger, cinder block room, dimly lit through wide, narrow openings near the ceiling. Chipped and rusted metal cribs lined the walls and newer ones created paths just wide enough for him to walk. Twenty toddlers stood blank-faced with tiny hands gripping the sides; others sat motionless in the deafening stillness. Some had obvious mental or physical handicaps; spina bifida, hydrocephalus, elephantiasis, Down syndrome. "Please do not talk to the children," the Sister directed. It appeared that no one ever did. She glanced at his camera, "And please, Doctor, do not be taking snaps."

"What happens to these children, Sister? Where do they go when they grow up?"

"They are never leaving," answered Sister Tia. "The healthy ones tend to the less fortunate."

A stifling bacterial stench like the odor of rotting food mixed with vomit, rat poison and Dettol disinfectant wafted from behind a heavy wooden door. Keir pushed the door open.

"This is where newcomers stay until they are happy to be here. We don't allow visitors in this area," she said pursing her lips. His foot prevented the Sister from closing the door. He pushed his way in.

The space reminded Keir of a kennel filled with dog crates. Each cage had a drain in the floor and a bucket for water. An internee could curl up on the crudely grouted floor; but even a small child could not stand or unfold. Near the back, a half-naked, emaciated child cowered in a cage, his gender obvious below a too-small faded shirt. The child lifted his gaze as if his shaved head were too heavy to hoist. Infected rat bites, swollen and red, dotted his ears, arms, and legs. His vacant eyes focused on nothing.

"We must be moving on," insisted Sister Tia.

As Keir backed out of the room, too disturbed to object, he added sleeping mats, ointment, and antibiotics to his mental list of supplies.

Each room housed increasingly older children, the age of the humans determining their fellow inmates. In the grassless court yard, shaded by the branches of a leafless tree, disabled adults sat in the dirt, or in wheel-less wheel chairs. Nearby, two older men sat in new wheel chairs. Their shoulders slumped as they drooled onto trousers that reeked of urine.

In the next room light through a narrow glass-less window near the ceiling outlined frail, bent, ancient residents slumped in chairs, staring at the nothingness. Others, supported by canes or walkers, trudged from wall to wall like zoo animals.

🐘 🐘 🐘

The next morning, Ashook drove Keir from store to store. Loaded with sleeping mats for the caged boy, medication for Sister Dilu, and other supplies, Keir knocked on the wooden door. Grateful for the supplies, Sister Tia reported that the caged boy had died in the night. Sister Dilu had also died.

Death was an imminent fact of life at the orphanage.

A few days later, when Keir told his fellow scientists about the deplorable conditions, they considered him as if he had been surprised that the sun came up that morning. Hunched by years of study, a frail elderly colleague with thick white hair and age-carved face, peered over his wire-frame glasses, "What did you expect Dr. Keefe, the Palace Hotel?"

chapter 9

First Adventure

Shakti's little head appeared by the garden wall. Her lice-infested hair leapt in sun-bleached coils.

Claire beckoned, "Come, sweetie, here's your lunch."

"Llll-un-ch" Shakti parroted as she climbed onto the bench.

As always, Claire washed the girl's hands and face and Shakti used her fingers to eat her meal. Claire ate with a white plastic fork. When they finished, Claire dropped the empty containers into the trash bin.

"I'm moving into my flat soon. Come, let's see if the maid has finished cleaning." It was their first adventure together beyond the wall of the hotel.

Chunks of sidewalk rose and fell as if poured by an earthquake. A man with no hands thrust a dirty plastic bucket toward Claire. Another begged, tugging at the hem of her skirt from the sidewalk while dirty bandages slid from leprosy lesions on his legs and arms.

Grit lifted into the sour air as buzzing and beeping traffic created the only breeze. Claire covered her mouth and nostrils with her scarf and held tight to Shakti's hand. They escaped into a small walled garden covered with passion flower vines. A splashing fountain muffled the clamor of scooters and perpetual honking of taxis, buses, and cars. Dappled sunlight shone through a Sandalwood tree.

Shakti hesitated, breathing in the passion flower scent. . . somehow familiar.

They climbed four flights of rough concrete stairs. Claire avoided the rickety, slow moving elevator. She had seen her neighbors trapped in the tiny box between floors and one occasion the contraption had plummeted three flights. Fortunately no one was seriously injured. Climbing was faster and safer. Claire unlocked the door and left Shakti on the landing, certain the child's apprehension would dissolve with curiosity.

When she stepped inside, Shakti ran her fingertips along the interior walls, her eyes wide. Her fingers traced sofa cushions. She followed Claire into the bedroom and touched the bare mattress. Claire sat down, fell back, and closed her eyes.

"Sleep," Shakti announced.

"Yes. Yes! How do you know that word?"

Claire led Shakti into the kitchen. When Claire turned on the tap, Shakti jumped, then reached her hand into the flow of cool water.

Claire turned up the hot water and Shakti laughed. This was the most magical thing she had ever experienced, flowing hot water.

They walked into the second bedroom. A doll, a teddy bear, and children's books spilled from hotel shopping bags. Shakti cocked her head like a curious puppy and Claire realized Shakti had never played with dolls or toys. Her life was entirely consumed with survival; rummaging for food, finding safe places to sleep, and seeking fountains where she could drink and splash away the grime.

"I'll bring you here again soon. We'll make the beds and unpack, but today, I need to get back to work."

As they reached the hotel, Shakti darted between the buildings to rejoin Radeeka and the others, and Claire slid into a taxi to the office.

🐘 🐘 🐘

On Saturday, Shakti and Claire returned to the flat together after lunch.

Giggling and dancing with absolute abandon, Shakti took her first shower as Claire sealed the red dress in a plastic garbage bag to contain the odor. She poured medicated shampoo into Shakti's hair and began to rub. Neither liked the smell.

Claire showed Shakti how to wash herself with a sweet-soapy washcloth. After a long time in the flowing warm water, Claire wrapped Shakti in a huge soft towel, hugged her, and placed her in front of a mirror. Claire stood next to her grinning and waving. Shakti began to understand. She touched the glass, her own face, and the glass again. She dropped the towel and stood in front of the mirror, fascinated and delighted. Claire wrapped a blue and yellow kerchief around the child's head hoping to contain the lice until she could cut the girl's hair. She helped Shakti into a new yellow dress. Shakti pushed the panties away, refusing to wear them.

Claire began unpacking her luggage, transferred to her flat by the hotel porter.

She hung up her dresses, blouses, and pants, tucked underwear into drawers, arranged her mascara, lipstick, and hairbrush on the tall dresser, and positioned her shoes on a rack in the closet. Shakti watched with fascination. She reached to touch the soft fabrics hanging in the closet.

Claire made her own bed, then Shakti followed her into the smaller room with a single bed. Claire hung little dresses in the closet, put little panties in the drawers and little sandals on the floor of the closet.

Together they made the bed. Claire placed a doll and teddy bear near the pillow, and games and books on nearby shelves. She watched Shakti walk around the bed, with her fingertips drifting along the soft lavender chenille bedspread. Shakti studied the doll's dress, shoes, and fair-skinned face. Its blue eyes opened and closed. Claire made a mental note to find a more appropriate, brown skinned doll with local-style clothing.

Claire served another meal as the sun went down and read a book aloud to Shakti, pointing to the words and pictures. Shakti fell asleep on the sofa, cuddled next to Claire.

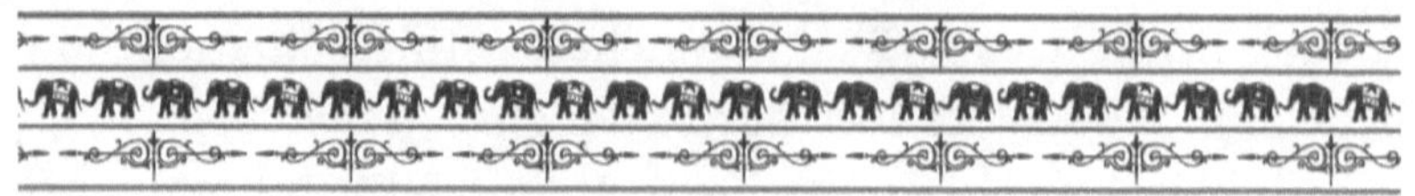

chapter 10

SHAKTI

Unable to stay away, I went back to the hotel without the others. I stood behind the wall as a red-haired man joined the blue-eyed woman on the bench. I could see the light between them and when he walked away, her light trailed after him like dust behind a truck.

One day she took me to where she stayed. She helped me shower and I learned to love the smell of soap. It was the first time I took a shower, the first time I used soap. She gave me a new yellow dress.

I watched Claire unpack her belongings. I had never worn panties or shoes but I knew what they were. Claire's bras, mascara, and lipstick were a complete mystery.

I fell asleep while she read to me. I didn't understand the language, but I loved curling up next to Claire; the sound of her voice, the smell of her. It was the first book I'd ever seen and the first time anyone read to me, the first time I slept in a bed.

Rose-colored light filled the room at day break. I took a few moments to remember I had fallen asleep while Claire read to me.

I had no thought of sneaking away from Claire. I enjoyed being with her, being clean, and having all the food I could eat, but Radeeka, Jamal, and the others were my family. As an independent person, never mind not yet four years old, I simply returned to the others.

While Claire slept, I stood on the landing by the golden treetops as the horizon changed from gold to clear blue. I marveled at the vastness of the sunrise. It was the first time I saw the horizon.

Breathing in the passion flower fragrance in the garden paradise, I listened to a big black bird perched in a sandalwood tree, k-eel, k-eel, k-eel. Its repetitive loud crack blended like drums with the songs of more colorful birds. Birds I had never seen, their music unfamiliar.

When I reunited with Radeeka and the others, she said, "Shakti, I was worried! I saw you with the yellow haired woman. Where did you sleep?"

"Her good name is Claire." My voice rose with the excitement of my adventure as I told Radeeka the story of the walled garden, the stairs, and the magical room where hot water streamed from the wall. She had told me stories of such places, but I thought her stories were fantasy. In those days I didn't know that Radeeka had once lived in a lovely flat with her own bedroom, her own bathroom, the housekeeper's cooking and her parent's love. I didn't know how much she missed them. I lacked the ability to articulate my feelings but I sensed something terrible had happened and that she struggled to reassemble her life. I felt the same deep sadness when I was with Claire.

Like a grown-up mother, Radeeka wanted to know how I knew it was safe to follow the foreign woman.

"Her light was very beautiful," I told her. "And I heard the music."

Radeeka was curious about the music I spoke of so often but it was difficult to explain. The sound was not like the music we heard coming from cars or buildings or the sitar and harmonium that accompanied the dancers in the park after dark. How could I explain the music I heard when it was unlike anything in my awareness, or hers? More than ten years later I heard the harp played for the first time, and realized the music in my heart could be duplicated and explained.

I have come to know that many children see auras and hear music, but as they grow up, either they outgrow the phenomenon or well-meaning adults teach them to hear and see "reality." Children forget what they knew at birth, and they learn to conform to the world around them. Partially due to the support of Keir, and Claire, I never lost my ability to see the colors and hear the music, and I always knew I wanted to help others heal.

chapter 11

RUNAWAY

"Doctor Keefe here," he answered the phone in a deep, sleepy voice.

"I'm sorry, did I wake you?"

"Claire? Are you alright? It's 6:00 am. . . Sunday!"

"I'm so sorry, I didn't think about the time, I just needed to talk to you."

"What's happened?" he said, sitting up, wide awake.

"I made a dreadful mistake. I brought Shakti to my flat and gave her a shower and shampooed the lice out of her hair and gave her a new dress and read to her and she fell asleep so I put her into the bed and now I woke up and she's gone, and . . . ."

"Slow down, breathe. I'll be right there."

Claire made a pot of coffee and paced the flat until Keir arrived less than fifteen minutes later.

"What was I thinking? I shouldn't have introduced everything all at once. I know better." Her arms waved around her as he stood on the landing. "She's never even slept in a bed before. I'm sure she's never been away from that older girl for more than an hour, and she's too little to be out there by herself." She pointed toward the street behind him.

"May I come in?" His warm expression revealed a heart filled with love and understanding.

"Yes, of course, I'm sorry," she stepped back so he could enter the short hallway.

"We'll sit down and talk about this rationally as soon as I have a cup of that coffee I smell, milk if you have it," he said.

She poured coffee into mugs painted with dancing Indian women and after stirring powdered milk into both, gave one to Keir. She took a deep shuddering breath. "Come, I'll give you a tour. Here's the room I fixed up for Shakti. Look, she tried to make her own bed, and she never even slept in a. . ."

"It's difficult to take your time when it's obvious she needs so much."

"I couldn't miss her anymore if she were. . . if. . ."

He hugged her. "Claire," he said, pulling back, "She didn't run away. She went home to the only family she knows. I can't begin to imagine what it would be like to wake up in a bed alone if you'd been sleeping on the street like a pack of puppies for as long as you could remember. And won't the older girl be worried and wonder what happened to her?"

"I didn't think of it that way. I just wanted to get her off the street, out of danger, but you're right."

"I'm certain she knows the way back to her pack. I suggest we wait until lunch and see if she appears at the fountain. Until then, do you fancy a drive to take you out of yourself? You need a distraction from both the office and Shakti. Ashook is just downstairs."

"That's a good idea," she said, reaching for a tissue. "I have a thermos, we can take coffee with us."

"I'll make another pot while you get dressed."

Claire wrapped her arms around her night gown. "How embarrassing."

"Not at all, now I know what to expect. . . ." He drew her to his chest and kissed her for the first time; a long, lingering, tender kiss. "I've been wanting to do that since the first time I saw you at the hotel."

"Me too," and she kissed him.

"But if you don't put some clothes on, well. . . ," he cleared his throat. "Ashook is waiting."

"Yes, of course. I'll be right out." She closed her bedroom door and emerged less than ten minutes later with damp hair, dressed in a long denim skirt and white cotton blouse with rolled up sleeves.

"I love a woman who doesn't dally," he laughed.

"And I love a man who makes coffee." She wanted to kiss him again, but she didn't.

"I filled the thermos. Let's go." Once again he put his palm in the small of her back, and the tension drained from her body. After his hand moved away, his energy remained there, reassuring her.

She grabbed her shopping basket on the way out.

🐘 🐘 🐘

The sun cast purplish shadows under blue tarps as they strolled Ashook's favorite market. Ashook helped them select the perfect mangoes, foot-long green beans, and potatoes, and led them to the baker-*wallah*. When the tandoori oven opened, the aroma of bread hovered for a lovely instant before the sour street scent returned.

"This will make a lovely dinner," she said looking into the basket. Thanks for your help, Ashook."

She smiled at Keir. "And thank you for helping me slow down and consider the reason Shakti left this morning."

"Happy to be of service."

They wandered through the market holding hands. Ashook hurried ahead to get the car.

Keir stood in the portico at the hotel while Claire waited on the bench. Perspiration trickled down her back, even in the shade. Shakti didn't appear.

"Try not to make too much of her absence today," said Keir. "I'm sure it has nothing to do with yesterday's adventure."

Ashook drove them back to the flat.

Together, they prepared the vegetables for dinner, "Where did you find wine? This is nice." She took another sip.

"When you've been in Mumbai as long as I have, you start to know such things." He laughed, "I admit, the hotel wine shop."

"Of course! What would we do without the hotel?" She quickly washed their plates and put them in the rack. "I'm learning to enjoy vegetables and ri. . . ?"

He locked her in a hug, and they moved to the bedroom.

Their first love making was slow, and tender. Neither shy nor inhibited, they leisurely explored, as if they had known each other forever.

The alarm clock buzzed at 6:00 am. "Do you always get up so early?" he said in a deep voice as he rolled over to hug her.

"Yes," she said, equally groggy.

"Why, might I ask?"

"I do my yoga practice before work. Reduces stress. Keeps me fit." She rolled on top of him, "Maybe I'll try a new pose this morning," she giggled.

"Splendid!"

chapter 12

THE OFFICE

Claire arrived at her office feeling fresh and clean. Getting ready in her own apartment, and riding to work in a lovely clean Mercedes, not to mention the early morning love-making, gave her morale a boost in spite of her concern for Shakti.

Throughout the morning, she managed to focus on the telecom network she was hired to launch.

Claire, Craig, and Tom stood in front of a map pinned to the conference room wall. Green shading identified parts of the city where Craig determined customers were more likely to pay for cellular service, including the Pune-Mumbai Highway. Yellow shading indicated secondary coverage requirements. Dots marked the locations the engineers identified as optimal for cell sites, red dots indicated no agreement had been signed and blue dots identified the land owners had signed contracts. There were only a few blue dots.

"How close are you to signing the other contracts?" Claire gestured toward the numerous red dots.

"Meetings are scheduled for this week with the owner of several of the target sites. We met with him during preliminary fact finding trips. He was interested and cooperative," the engineer said as he pointed to the map.

"I was hoping we'd be farther along by now but I'm aware of the difficulties. . ." they all nodded, "Ah, well, just keep pushing. I'd like a list of the property owners when you have a chance."

"I'll print one out for you as soon as I get the printer working again," said Tom.

Fifteen minutes later Claire and Craig met with a local PR consultant to discuss the launch.

Shiny black hair filled with pomade and dandruff flakes clung to Mr. Gupta's scalp. He wore a rumpled business suit and his shirt was food stained. "I must be saying, I have never been meeting such a beautiful Chief Officer. I hope you are enjoying shopping in India," he gushed.

Claire had discovered that Indian men were unaccustomed to meeting blonde American women, and inexperienced with women in charge of a huge technical project. She took a deep breath and tried not to show her disgust.

"Tell me about your PR experience, Mr. Gupta," said Claire, with a tone of harsh formality.

"Oh, I am being very excellent at selling all kinds of goods," he said.

"Can you provide us with examples of PR programs you've developed for local businesses?"

His face remained blank.

"I mean Public Relations campaigns, articles for magazines, billboards, stories on radio or TV? What companies have you promoted?"

The meeting lasted less than fifteen minutes.

"Why did you waste my time with that guy? He doesn't have a clue!" said Claire after Mr. Gupta left. "Can't we find a local PR candidate who doesn't start the meeting with an insult?"

"Don't count on it," said Craig. "I've interviewed several applicants. He's just an example. Public Relations, as we know it, doesn't exist here."

"I'll give you a few more weeks, but we might need to bring in some help. I know a dynamite PR consultant in Boston who could train some smart local graduates. Her father was born in India and she's spent a lot of time in Mumbai. She can hit the ground running."

"Based on what I've seen so far, there's no point in waiting. Get her over here. We'll start recruiting at the University of Mumbai and maybe the college in Pune too. If she gets here in time, we can recruit before graduation."

Julie, the general manager of customer service, asked Claire to interview a candidate for call center manager. This hire would be more difficult than a PR position and just as important. Local candidates had no experience in call center management; most didn't understand the purpose of a call center.

The telecommunication system Claire and her company were building would connect India seamlessly to the rest of the world via the Internet. Unaware that soon companies across the United States would be routing their customer service calls to India, they were pioneering the local call center industry. The people Claire's staff hired and trained would be the first in India to have experience, and would eventually become managers and trainers for call centers providing customer service for companies across the world.

The candidate they hired was smart and eager, but he

had a lot to learn before taking over the customer service department. She made plans to send him to Seattle so he could see a call center in action and addend additional training.

Her watch read 6:15 pm. Shakti would have come and gone, if she came to the fountain at all.

Before leaving, she sent a fax to her manager in Seattle requesting additional staff for PR including the name of the candidate she hoped would agree to a short assignment in India.

Claire couldn't decide what was worse, the hot, crowded sidewalk or a smoldering taxi filled with garlic and curry body odor. As she stepped from the taxi by her flat, Ashook's Mercedes turned the corner, and Keir emerged from the back seat. "I hope this isn't presumptuous of me. Ashook took me to the market. I brought groceries for dinner," he said with a grin. "You look absolutely spiffy in that *kurta*."

Claire was still uneasy wearing the local outfits she'd purchased in the hotel dress shop. The *kurtas* were bulky over the drawstring *salwar* pants and the six foot, scarf-like *dupattes* were annoyingly difficult to manage, often getting stuck in drawers and doors, but clothes were essential for her credibility at the office as more locals joined the team. Walking around without a *dupatte* would be the same as walking around half dressed. "Did you see Shakti at lunch time?"

"Yes, she and the other children were chased from the fountain again. I managed to give her my leftovers and a couple of extra meals before they fled."

"That's good. I hardly had time to worry, my day was so busy," said Claire.

He handed plastic grocery bags to Claire and retrieved his briefcase and duffel from the back seat, "That will be all tonight, Ashook. Please pick us up at half eight in the morning."

"Yes sir." Ashook drove away smiling.

"I was wondering what I would have for dinner," she said as Keir leaned down for a kiss. "What did you bring?"

"Vegetables, rice, and chapatti. What else?"

"Every culture on the planet must have their own version of a tortilla or crepe. I'm actually beginning to like them. I'll be out in a jiff." She disappeared into her room, emerging in less than ten minutes in a purple and yellow loose-fitting sun-dress, her hair damp from a quick shower.

He handed her a glass of Chardonnay. "Shakti looked around for you but didn't hesitate to take the food from me." Keir pulled a bulging manila folder from his briefcase and put it on the table. "I visited the Central Adoption Resource Authority, CARA, this afternoon after class."

She touched the folder with her fingertips as if it held a bomb that might explode.

As tenderly as he could, he said, "Claire, you can't bring a street child into your home like an abandoned kitten. It doesn't work that way."

"I didn't consider legal rights, I was thinking of Shakti, out there eating garbage, and sleeping where she could be kidnapped and sold for who knows what. How can any logical person object to that?"

"Logical people have nothing to do with it. We're talking about government bureaucracy." He stood behind her with his arms around her. She leaned her back against his chest as she opened a folder. "You'll need to apply to the authorities and according to the chap I talked with today, getting their help could take a year or more. I have the applicable forms here," he said with his chin on her shoulder.

"A year! That's absurd."

"There's a bigger problem. You'll need a No Objection Certificate signed by her legal guardian. She's not available for adoption if no one has the right to give her up. . . Don't look at me that way—I'm just telling you what I learned," he said as she spun to face him.

Avoiding his eyes, she said, "I'm sorry. I appreciate your efforts. I really do. You are amazing. Thank you." She leaned her forehead on his chest and took a deep breath. "You're aware by now that I didn't get where I am by taking no for an answer."

🐘 🐘 🐘

Claire was surprised to see the Recognized Indian Placement Agency official's office. He ranked high in RIPA but his corner office was dark and shabby. Bundles of dusty files tied with twine rose to eye-level in all corners of his office as well as on the edge of his dented metal desk. The wide-open and screen-less second floor windows invited dust, noise, flies, and exhaust fumes.

They sat across the desk from Mr. Achara. His unruly henna dyed hair revealed gray at the scalp. His belly hung over his dusty trousers. A chill went up Claire's spine in the brief moment he looked at her with his menacing and sinister honey-gold eyes.

"I'm interested in adopting a little girl," Claire said with as much authority as she could muster.

Mr. Achara looked at Keir as if Keir had spoken the words. "I have a list of agencies with available children. Of course, these children are mostly girls." The disdainful tone when he said girls made it clear that he had no regard for any female, girl or woman. "Did you want to adopt a baby or an older child?" he said to Keir.

"You don't understand, Mr. Achara," said Claire

placing her palms on the gritty desk, leaning forward. "I have befriended a street child. I would like to adopt her."

"Have you discussed this with the child's parents?" he said, still looking at Keir.

"She has no parents! She lives on the street!" Claire's voice became shrill and Keir patted her knee under the desk.

Tourists frequently came to Mr. Achara's office, wanting to adopt a child, like a souvenir. He could not hold his temper. His voice grew harsh, "Where is this child you speak of?"

Claire hesitated, "She lives on the street. . . ."

Keir stood up abruptly and shook the official's hand. "Thank you Mr. Achara, you've been most helpful. We will give the idea further consideration."

"Yes, of course." He handed Keir a stained sheet of paper. "Here is the list of agencies that deal with international adoptions. Contact one of them if you decide to adopt before returning to England." He still didn't acknowledge Claire.

"I had a dreadful feeling when he asked where to find Shakti," Claire said as they got into the car.

"I suspect that neither the authorities nor hotel management wants a band of street children harassing tourists, and, sorry to say, we look like tourists," Keir agreed. "Your *salwar* outfit doesn't make much difference considering the color of your eyes and hair."

"So how can we find a legal way to get her off the street without alarming the authorities?" Claire's voice was shrill again.

Ashook watched them in the rear view mirror. He couldn't help hearing the conversation. Personal experience had taught Ashook that rescue was possible. He didn't want to say anything yet, but would discuss the situation with his uncle. He hoped to bring good news to his boss within a few day's time.

🐘 🐘 🐘

Claire asked her secretary if anyone she knew had adopted a child.

"It is being very expensive to be adopting a child in Mumbai," offered Janus.

After dinner Claire asked Keir, "Do you think that Mr. Achara expects me to offer graft?"

"I'm sure payments will be made before any agreement can be reached, but it's too early in the process. We must follow rules established by the authorities," he said, sorting through the documents. "From everything I've read so far, the government would sooner commit children to that dreadful institution than allow a foreigner to provide foster care, never mind adoption."

"But she's out there somewhere. Drives me insane." Claire poured another glass of wine.

While having coffee at Claire's flat the next morning, Keir began reading a newspaper from the bottom of a stack in Claire's living room, while she made scrambled eggs for their breakfast. "Did you see this article? It's an old paper."

"I'm so behind on local news. I saved those papers thinking I'd find time to catch up," she shrugged.

"A few months ago, police found the wife of the RIPA official we met with, Mr. Achara, washed up on Dargah Road, near the Haji Ali Mosque. They expect that his three-year-old daughter also drowned. His new-born son is left without a mother." Keir read aloud, "Mr. Achara's sister-in-law also died recently in a kitchen fire. She is survived by three young sons. Mr. Achara had no comment."

"I wonder if he had a hand in either death," she said in a deep sarcastic voice.

"The article stops short of accusing him, but I wouldn't put it past the old sod. He's as cold as ice with no regard for women."

chapter 13

THE RAID

*I*ntimidating hot wind whipped through the canyon of buildings, too far from the sea for benefit. The gluey, menacing air closed around Claire as she stepped from the car, the wind nearly shoving her off balance. People on the street rushed more than usual, as if out-racing the approaching monsoon storm. Her blue and yellow *salwar kameez* whipped around her as she fought the wind gusts and hurried the short distance from the car to the office. She nearly lost her yellow *dupatte* for the first time that day.

The office was unnervingly quiet, empty except for her secretary. The rest of her staff was running late. Janus was there no matter how early Claire arrived in the morning and remained every afternoon no matter how late Claire left. She always looked professional alternately wearing the same two *salwar* outfits.

Claire planned to finish her monthly report and fax it to her boss in Seattle but she fought with the printer, having to reboot several times before the report emerged. When she tried to fax it to Seattle, the fax would not connect.

With the thirteen and one half hour time difference, it would be on his desk when he came in the next morning, if she could get it to go through.

The ubiquitous dust meant peril to all technical equipment causing computers, fax machines and printers to malfunction. The switch room was built with three air-locked entries. All visitors were required to pass through all three chambers wearing white overalls over their clothing with shower cap–like hats over their hair and beards. No exceptions.

The system they were building would technologically leapfrog worldwide communication systems, bringing basic telephony, cellular, and Internet service through an advanced wireless network. Since telephone service in India was still in its infancy, and Internet was non-existent, the wireless system would make installation of telephone poles and lines unnecessary. Before arriving, the team members had been encouraged by the opportunity of a life-time.

Their enthusiasm subsided, however, when they realized the magnitude of the project in a place where electricity, clean water, and sewage treatment were luxurious amenities. Claire felt as if they were building the Golden Gate Bridge over a trickling creek.

As the local staff grew, Claire learned that yes was the answer to every polar question. If she said, *Can you finish this today?* whether laundry at the hotel or a report at the office, the answer was always yes, but if she said, *How long will it take to finish this?* the answer might be two days' time.

As the Chief Executive Officer, she couldn't expect fifty or sixty hours per week from her highly paid expat team. In Boston, long hours were not unusual for a high-profile start-up project like this one, but in India her staff needed time away from the office. Finding safe food to eat, recovering from heat exhaustion, and sudden onset of Delhi belly were all part of the assignment.

Tom, the Chief Engineer leaned into her office, "Got a minute?"

"Sure Tom, what's up?"

"Yesterday I had a meeting with the local land owner I told you about; apparently he owns half of Mumbai," he sprawled on the chair by Claire's desk. "When I met with him during preliminary fact finding trips, he appeared cooperative. He still seems cooperative but we aren't getting anywhere. Every time we meet to sign papers, he finds additional points to negotiate. At this rate, we'll never get the system up and running."

"Do you think he expects some sort of bribe or graft?"

"Geez, I didn't think of that," said Tom.

"We can't participate in such customs, and I won't break any laws, but. . . there must be a way. . ." She leaned back, "I have no idea how, but I'll figure it out."

Claire directed Janus to keep trying the fax machine, and took a taxi through the steaming streets to lunch at the hotel. The air was slightly cooler when the rain subsided but 100% humidity left her wet with perspiration.

She shivered more than usual when she entered the air-conditioned hotel. She ordered an omelet with naan. While she waited, the children rounded the wall toward the fountain. Immediately, the hotel manager burst from the lobby, waving his arms, shouting, "Arrest them! Arrest them!"

Two policemen surrounded the fountain. One grabbed Jamal who was almost more than the officer could manage and the other grabbed Shakti by the hair but missed Radeeka by a thread. Claire ran through the lobby and reached the wall just as naked Shakti was tossed like a sack of potatoes into what looked like a 1940s paddy wagon.

Claire ran into traffic behind the vehicle shouting "Stop, wait, where are you taking her?" Stone sized rain drops distorted her vision. Her yellow *dupatte* flowed behind her, then drifted upward like a kite's tail caught by the wind. Auto-rickshaws, buses, taxis, scooters, bicycles, and ox carts surrounded her. For an instant Shakti's eyes peered at her from between the bars of the dark truck, her little fingers holding the bars. Horns honked, people shouted in Hindi and Marathi as traffic closed around Claire.

A tiny auto-rickshaw driver stopped next to Claire. A long white beard, stained with streaks of red paan juice, tickled his bony bare chest. His teeth were also stained red but his elf-like eyes sparkled with warmth and understanding. He assisted Claire into his little vehicle, and drove her back to the hotel entrance. Noisy rickshaws were forbidden from entering the hotel grounds so he parked by the entrance, helped her onto the sidewalk, and bowed, hoping for payment.

In a daze, Claire walked to Shakti's yellow dress and rocked it like a baby. With surreal curiosity, she stared at the crush of humanity going about their business beyond the wall. *How can they hurry through their lives as if nothing has happened?*

Holding a huge red and white umbrella, the hotel manager paid the driver and escorted Claire into the cold lobby. "Madam, those dirty beggar children will not be bothering you any longer."

She looked at him. His face swirled as her legs collapsed under her.

She awoke an hour later on Keir's bed with a blood pressure cuff squeezing her arm.

"What's going on? Where am I? Did Shakti get her lunch?"

"You fainted in the lobby just as I came through the door. I saw you running through the rain and traffic but I was too far away to help. Thank heaven for that rickshaw driver."

Claire removed the cold cloth from her forehead, "Did a policeman throw Shakti into a paddy wagon, or was that a terrible nightmare?"

"It is a nightmare, but it happened."

"We need to find her." She tried to sit up but fell back.

"I think I know where they took her, but you can't come with me."

"Indeed I can," she insisted, though weakly.

"I'll find someone to stay with you," he said, checking her pulse again.

"How absurd, I'm fine."

Keir called the front desk and within minutes, an American woman dressed in a white nurse's uniform knocked on the door. "Hello Judy. Claire has had a trauma. She'll be fine but I need someone to stay with her until my return."

"Yes, of course. Dr. Keefe."

He sat on the edge of the bed taking Claire's pulse, and poured her a glass of ayurvedic tea. "This will help you rest. I make it with Brahmi and honey. You stay here with your feet up and Judy will keep the compresses cold until your fever and blood pressure go back down. I promise I will find Shakti. I promise!"

chapter 14

INSIDE THE WALL

I saw the hotel manager spring from the lobby door with a bright, dangerous glow around him. Before I could run, a policeman grabbed me from behind. One moment I folded my dress and the next moment the policeman carried me toward a truck. He threw me in and I landed on my naked rump.

Another policeman threw Jamal in with me and slammed the door.

Holding the bars, I saw Radeeka running away from the hotel. Thankful that she had avoided capture. Then I saw Claire chasing the truck into traffic. Soon the cars and rickshaws closed around her. Rain fell like a gauze curtain. When the truck turned, I tumbled sideways onto Jamal. We sat in the dark, back to back supporting each other as the trunk crisscrossed through traffic. Jamal's head was bleeding, he said nothing. He had frightened us with stories of his experiences in jail and I was certain we were both going there now.

I felt his trembling body. The music in my heart grew louder, I hoped loud enough for Jamal to feel its soothing energy. I began chanting Radeeka's mantra, aham prema, ahan prema. He joined me and the tension in his body eased.

The truck suddenly stopped. Jamal almost rolled out when bright sunlight split the dark interior. One policeman pushed Jamal further inside, as the other grabbed me by the hair and jerked me to the ground. I heard Jamal shout, "Namaste, Shakti, dhanyavaad," and I knew he had felt the music. The cop dragged me across the street, past a stone wall, through an open wooden door and locked me in a wire cage. The wooden door slammed shut and the truck sped away. I never saw Jamal again.

Squatting naked on the rough stones, I lapped water like a cow from a big bucket. Wiping my chin with the back of my arm, I looked up to see a nun frowning at me through the bars. Light through a narrow horizontal window high on the wall behind her made her white sari glow, but the nun was not an angel. She opened the cage gate, pulled me out by the arm, and began shaving my head with a dry razor. Blood trickled down my face from several nicks. She washed my body with a coarse sponge and Dettol disinfectant, meant for cleaning floors. The lather stung, especially the back of my legs and heels where the policeman had dragged me across the rough concrete. She hosed off the disinfectant, pulled a dirty dress over my wet body, and shoved me back into the cage. She said nothing.

Afternoon sun turned the stone wall orange. The still air became hotter than the street. I fell asleep on the rough wet floor until the smell of rice woke me. I extended my arm through the bars but the bowl was just beyond my reach. As I stretched to reach it, the nun took the bowl away.

The room became darker than any place I'd ever been. Deep shadows hid my toes and the stone wall muffled the sounds of the city. I heard the rat's feet scratching on the stones all around me and felt the tickle of their claws on my legs.

Again, I chanted Radeeka's mantra. At the sound of the first note, the rats fled. With my legs crossed and my hands resting on my knees, palms up, I breathed deeply. . . I entered the golden garden. Fresh air blew my long, well brushed hair and a sparkling river splashed over rocks. I smelled passion fruit blossoms as a misty canopy reflected the rose hew of sunrise. I listened to the magical healing music only I could hear. In this safe place, I was neither hungry nor afraid.

A day went by before the nun let me eat the rice she teased me with. She dumped the contents of a small bowl onto the floor and I devoured it like a wild dog. In the seven days stay, she never spoke to me.

I squatted over the keyhole toilet then splashed myself with water from the bucket. I tried to wash away the smell of diarrhea but the odor remained. The bucket was left empty for a day. When she added only a few inches of water, I had to tip the bucket to drink.

chapter 15

JAMAL'S BRIEF LIFE

Keir vowed to rescue Shakti from the orphanage. Mr. Hamadani promised to find Radeeka and bring her home.

No one saved Jamal.

Jamal's mother gave birth in a cardboard box in Dharavi, the largest slum in Mumbai, not far from the airport, where a million people lived on one square mile of recovered swamp land. She was a homeless thief who sold recyclables when she could and her body when necessary. She used her baby boy to elicit sympathy. Her usual territory included the entrance to the airport, where she begged for rupees exiting tourists could not exchange for other currency. Jamal and his mother had been arrested several times, taken to the precinct, and thrown into a crowded cell. Officers took turns on Jamal's mother, seized every rupee she had, then released them.

When Jamal was five and no longer an adorable little traffic stopper, his mother left him asleep on a sidewalk.

Jamal had been arrested several times. The policemen beat him. His cell mates tortured him with unspeakable acts of violence before he was let go. The next arrest, when he was almost ten, he was lined up with the other prisoners to be taken to Author Road Jail. Jamal was so thin, he pulled out of the handcuffs and ran. He met Radeeka a few days later, still wearing the blood caked clothing.

After the raid on the hotel fountain, the cop drop-kicked Jamal from the paddy wagon to the precinct holding cell where brutal criminals waited for transfer to Author Road Jail.

"Who's this little fucker?" said a perspiring, shirtless man, so filled with rage his eyes shone red. His bare foot kicked Jamal in ribs already broken by the policeman.

This time, Jamal could not escape the blue prison truck to Author Road Jail. Fear dried his mouth as the truck's dark interior cloaked his view of other prisoners towering above him. He trembled like a little mouse in a box full of king cobras. He tried to summon the sound that Shakti shared with him in the paddy wagon but his spirit was fading. His body had survived the brutality on more than one occasion. He knew he would not survive The Road.

On the inside, led by the red-eyed brute from the Mumbai precinct, the new inmates took turns kicking Jamal back and forth across the slimy floor like an airless soccer ball. The squat toilet oozed into a stinking swamp, leaving prisoners sitting in the brown sludge and Jamal coated with muck. Convicted murders with life sentences were assigned to guard duty. They created their own set of rules.

With a sinister smile, one such guard pushed a broken broom handle through the bars, "teach the little fucker a lesson," he said in a gravelly voice filled with mirth. He laughed aloud as the angry red-eyed prisoner beat every inch of ten-year-old Jamal. He bled from head lacerations and from every orifice; mouth, nose, eyes, ears, and anus.

Like recycled newspaper, Jamal's corpse was tossed to the curb with the bodies of other prisoners who could not survive the brutality of The Road. They were loaded onto a bullock drawn by black water buffalo and taken for a low cost sky burial on a mountain top outside of Mumbai.

chapter 16

RESCUE

Holding his worn leather doctor's satchel, Keir knocked but the big wooden doors of the orphanage didn't open. He pounded again and again, the sound echoing off the surrounding buildings. No one answered.

"The nuns won't open the door," Keir told Ashook. "I think I know a way to get their attention."

Ashook drove Keir back to the hotel.

Keir dashed through the lobby to the elevator and down the long hall to his suite.

He found Nurse Judy reading a paperback book next to the bed where Claire slept.

Keir removed the cloth and put his hand on Claire's forehead, and took her pulse. "It's back to normal, that's good, but keep the cold compresses going. I need to go back out. When she wakes up, have her drink more Brahmi tea."

"She keeps muttering in her sleep doctor, something about Lisa."

He had no time to consider who Lisa might be. "Can you stay longer?"

"Yes of course, doctor."

He traded his doctor's satchel for his briefcase and a newspaper. "If I don't come back before morning, please encourage her to drink the tea and order breakfast for both of you. I won't be gone that long, I hope." He dashed back to the elevator.

While Ashook drove, Keir tore the newspaper into rupee-sized strips. He made a stack about the size of his weekly donation and stuffed it into a brown paper bag.

Ashook parked on the dark side of the street. Keir walked the shadows until he reached the basket where he had deposited his weekly donation for the past three years. The hinges screeched as he opened the small gate. He put the brown paper bag filled with newspaper strips in the basket and waited in the dark for it to be retrieved. He was sure the screeching hinges would notify the nuns. When a hairy arm appeared, he grabbed it by the wrist. In a harsh voice filled with anger and concern, Keir said, "If you want my rupees, sir, you will open the door at once." He snatched the decoy away from the long fingered hand, released his grip, and waited by the wooden doors. Heavy footsteps grew louder until the doors opened, back-lighting a priest in a long black robe. "Good ee-va-neng," said the priest. "I. am. Father. Adesh."

"Good evening, Father. I would like to see Sister Tia."

"Sister Tia is being reassigned to an order in Calcutta, but your donation is very much appreciated." His long bony fingers uncurled and gestured toward the paper bag.

"I am Doctor Keir Keefe. I would like to check the health of your newcomers."

"I am sorry sir, the orphanage is closed to visitors," said the priest in a low, hoarse voice. "Now that Sister Dilu has passed, I am enforcing the rules here."

"I must check the health of the newcomers," Keir insisted. As he pushed past the priest, a pair of tall, pasty-skinned brutes appeared in the shadows. Their eyes glowed pink in the dim light. Each wore a white lungi with the fabric drawn up between his legs and tucked at the waist to look like pants. With grotesquely huge heads, arms like oak branches and abdomens rippling with muscle, they lifted Keir off the floor. The brown bag fell at Father Adesh's feet as he jerked his head toward the door. The albino twins tossed Keir into the street like a bag of trash.

"This is madness!" Keir screamed as Ashook ran across the street to help him to his feet.

"I am sorry, sir. Perhaps my family can help with your situation," said Ashook.

"Tell me more Ashook." Keir used his handkerchief to wipe the blood and dirt from his hands and face.

🐘 🐘 🐘

When a bloodied Keir returned to his hotel suite, Nurse Judy gathered first aid supplies from Keir's old medical satchel. As she began to clean and bandage the abrasions, "Good grief! What happened?"

"I ran into a priest and his frightful thugs. How's Claire?"

"She woke up for a while. I persuaded her to drink a cup of your brahmi tea. She took a shower, put on one of your shirts and went back to sleep. Seeing these bandages might not help her blood pressure."

"Indeed! . . . Did she talk in her sleep again?" he said as he poured Scotch into a small glass.

"Yes, quite a lot. She was trying to help someone named Lisa."

He pulled English pounds from his pocket and handed

the bills to her. "Thank you, Judy, you were a big help tonight."

"My pleasure doctor. Thank you. Let me know if you need anything more."

Keir downed his Scotch, took a long hot shower, then stretched his stiff body on the bed next to Claire. He touched her forehead. Her fever was down.

She opened her eyes, and rolled onto her side, strangely calm at the sight of his bandages. "Keir, what's going on?" Her voice was deeper than usual. "I dreamed that Shakti was thrown into a cage and you were tossed into the street like rubbish."

The authenticity of her dream seemed normal to him in light of the day's events. "How do you feel?"

"Really weird. Exhausted. Sort of out of body, surreal dreams, very strange. I can see that truck speeding away, the cars, bicycles, ox carts, and horns honking all around me, and little Lis...—I mean—Shakti staring out from between the bars like a captured mongrel. Where did they take her?"

"I suspect she's at the Catholic orphanage."

"That dismal place with the stone wall? They say no one ever leaves."

"It's worse now, if that's possible. The old nun who ran it for a thousand years did her best to take care of everyone but she died not long ago and a beastly priest has taken charge. His monstrous thugs threw me into the street."

Claire touched the bandage on his forehead as he went on.

"I'm worried about his motives. One of my colleagues said the orphanage has always enhanced revenue by offering child labor to the local economy. Now, with that Priest in charge, it can only get worse."

"My God, I hope it's just labor he's offering," she said.

"I've heard stories of child prostitution rings in this city." She shivered.

"I'll go mad if I think about such things happening to Shakti. Ashook offered to help. His family runs the restaurant where we had dinner." He smiled remembering their first date. "Ashook told me that his uncle and auntie might know how to get Shakti out of the orphanage. He's arranged for us to have dinner with them in a few days' time."

🐘 🐘 🐘

On Sunday evening, Keir picked up Claire for dinner.

"You look exceptionally handsome tonight," she said, when she opened the door. Keir wore a raw silk *kurta*, custom-made in deep green reminiscent of the moon-lit hills of Ireland. His red hair shone like sunset.

"And you are beautiful as always," He kissed her cheek. As they walked to the car, he said, "I'm sure you've learned that business customs in India are quite different from what you're accustomed to in the US."

"Of course, I run into Indian business customs every day. Most of the men don't know what to do with an American female in charge of a multi-million dollar project."

"I suspect our meeting tonight will be more difficult than your typical encounters," said Keir. "We can expect the uncle to take charge of the conversation while you and the auntie listen." He felt her stiffen but went on, "It may take more than one meeting to actually discuss the real issue at hand. We must follow their customs." He squeezed her hand. "Please don't be insulted."

"I understand. I don't like it, but I understand. I won't try to take charge. I'll do whatever it takes to help Shakti, but I'll go crazy if she isn't rescued soon."

As they made their way to the table, Claire walked

slightly behind Keir, wearing a rose-colored *salwar kameez.* Gold and green metallic embroidery circled the cuffs and square neckline. The *kameez* dress, slit to her hip, fell below her knees over tight-legged white *salwar* pants, elegantly bunched above white sandals. A gold barrette secured her blonde hair, scooped off the nape of her neck, more out of cool comfort than fashion. A hand painted *dupatte* draped around her throat and floated behind her. The geometric designs glistened in the candlelight like precious emeralds set in shimmering gold.

They made a striking couple among the otherwise local patrons. Heads turned.

Ashook introduced Keir and Claire to his auntie, Chachi, and his uncle, Chacha, who stood to greet them. Ashook backed into the shadows.

Chacha had thick white hair, a wide smile and wore a white shirt, white pants, and a long, dark blue Nehru vest.

A thick salt and pepper braid swung over her shoulder as Chachi stood with the assistance of her husband. She wore a blue and green sari and her big smile was quick and genuine. Her glimmering *mangalsutra* necklace was made of thick gold filigree and onyx beads and the *bindi* between her brows matched the blue of her sari. The vermilion *sindoor* powder in the part of Chachi's hair glowed in the dim candle light but Claire had yet to learn its meaning.

Chacha and Chachi had considerable influence in Mumbai; however, beneath the strong bureaucratic character, Keir detected a love for humanity that he never felt among his colleagues. Chachi carried herself with confidence and power, shaking his hand firmly, and looking him squarely in the eye, but as Keir predicted, her husband led the conversation throughout the meal. The women listened attentively.

Claire was not fond of remaining in the periphery, but she followed Chachi's lead, allowing the men to dominate. Chachi and Chacha effortlessly used pieces of naan to scoop the rice and sauces cooked by their staff. Claire managed eating with one hand, grateful that she had eaten here once before.

Claire's heart was breaking as she held her hand under the flow of warm water from the Sikh's pitcher. Not a word had been said about Shakti or the orphanage during their meal.

"Would you like to come inside for brandy?" Chachi invited as she dried her hand with the white towel.

Claire was hopeful again.

Young women, who could have been their daughters, dressed in western-style white blouses and jeans, served brandy, and left the room as the adults settled onto beautiful brocade upholstered sofas. The four talked and laughed like old friends. Claire began to see commonality, regardless of their diverse nationalities.

"When I married Chacha, I was a professor in the public health department at the university. Do you enjoy working there?" said Chachi.

"Immensely," said Keir. They discussed the joys of teaching college students and Keir's interest in studying alternative forms of healing.

Chachi nodded with a smile. She knew there would be talk of energy healing in the coming days.

Chacha was curious about Claire's job. "We understand you work for an American corporation here in Mumbai?"

"Yes, we're building a telecom system that will revolutionize communications in Mumbai. The system will provide cellular service and Internet, and of course, jobs for local people."

"Do you find it difficult working in India?" asked Chacha, speaking to Claire directly.

"To be honest, yes. We've hired some wonderfully intelligent people, and they are eager to learn and succeed. Getting contracts signed, however, has proven to be a challenge. It seems that negotiations never end."

"Ah yes, contracts are difficult in Mumbai. I have dealt with such matters for many years." He went on to tell them about the cement franchise he inherited from his uncle when he was just twenty-two. "Perhaps I can lend a hand with contract negotiations, but first, Ashook tells us you have a special friend being held at the orphanage."

Keir jumped in. "Claire had been giving her food. She hoped to adopt the child and get her off of the street but Indian adoption laws are difficult. I tried to help and arranged a meeting with an adoption official. A few days after our meeting, the police apprehended the child along with a little boy. The rest of the pack scattered. It's sickening to think that our meeting could have triggered the raid. I suspect they took her to the Catholic orphanage."

"I'm certain the timing of her capture was a coincidence. The hotel conducts such raids periodically when the young beggars get too comfortable in the fountain. The manager thinks that patrons are repulsed by the dirty children." Chacha stood. "Tomorrow afternoon we will find her." He motioned for Ashook. They all said good night.

Claire and Keir rode in silence while Keir considered a return to the orphanage and another encounter with Father Adesh.

"Ashook, thank you. Thank you, for giving us hope."

Ashook held the car door for her. "You are welcome, madam."

Ashook understood Shakti's plight more than they knew.

The following afternoon, Ashook drove into the hotel portico and Keir slid into the backseat with Chacha.

"I have arranged for a tour of the orphanage," said Chacha. "We will persuade the nuns to let us into the forbidden newcomers' area. I'm certain your little friend is in one of their deplorable cages."

"I've seen the cages in what they call the newcomers' area. Why do they confine the children like rabid dogs?" Keir asked Chacha.

"It is considered a breaking-in process. Street children are thought to be feral, not quite human. In India, cows and rats enjoy more respect than feral children, especially so for little girls. The nuns confine them, and when the children are allowed to enter the general population at the orphanage, the nuns expect them to be docile and obedient. . . if they survive."

"But there is nothing wild about that baby girl. Shakti is the kindest, most appreciative spirit I've ever encountered. She would share her only grain of rice," Keir said.

Keir had studied feral children. He knew how their minds worked, never reflecting on the past, never hoping for a better future. They were not conditioned to consider the future or what could have been different in their lives in the past or how things should be different in the future. They savored spoiled rice, drank dirty water, while living in the present moment, whatever the moment brought.

In his meditation practice, Keir struggled to be present, to quiet his mind, to relax his thoughts to stillness. These children didn't need to learn to let go of control because they had never had control of anything, ever.

Being caged without food and water became just another situation they had no control over. However, when their lives became unendurable in the present moment, some died in the cage.

Keir's stomach knotted as Chacha knocked and the big wooden door opened, but Father Adesh and his red-eyed albino thugs didn't appear. A nun he'd never seen led their tour from room to room. At last, Uncle requested in Hindi, "We would like to check the health of your newcomers."

"This is not possible," the nun replied. "We do not allow visitors. You understand. . ."

In a calm voice, in English words, Chacha said, "Dr. Keefe has donated generously." He gestured toward Keir. "He will continue to do so." Then in a demanding, stern tone, "Now take us to the newcomers without delay."

Keir trembled with relief when he saw Shakti huddled in the corner on the rough stone floor. Her shaved head tilted only slightly so she could stand up in the cage. She put her tiny hands on the bars and Keir knelt to match her palm to palm, the bars between them.

"Namaste" she said confidently. Everyone heard.

"Namaste, my dear Shakti," Keir said. "I have come to take you from this place." He added, "Claire sends her love."

Recognition in Shakti's eyes revealed that she understood.

"We will be taking the child with us," Chacha demanded in English. His stern voice echoing off the dark stone walls.

The nun responded, "But sir, she is being a young feral child, not yet tamed, not ready to be working in your household."

"I will be the judge of that." He gestured toward the door with a bulging envelope and she unlocked the cage.

Keir scooped up Shakti and hurried to the car. She was dreadfully emaciated but strong considering her ordeal.

Shakti slept curled up on Keir's lap during the hour-long ride. Inside the gates at Bhojan Thali, Ashook drove past the restaurant to a large two-story building Keir hadn't noticed before. A young woman, wearing jeans and a light blue t-shirt with a GAP logo waited in the portico. Her ponytail fell like liquid ink from a silver barrette high on the back of her head. She lowered her gaze, as the car slowed next to her. Keir was aware that Ashook became nervous and distracted at the sight of the beautiful young woman.

Shakti's scrawny arms clung to Keir's neck and her spindly legs hugged his waist as he got out of the car. She calmed on his shoulder as the young woman's loving energy met them like a gentle tropical breeze. "*Swagatam*, Shakti," said the young woman, "Welcome."

"You will be safe here, Shakti," Chacha said in Hindi, patting her back. "This is Neela, your new auntie. She will take care of you and be with you every minute as long as you need her. Keir and Claire can visit anytime."

"There is no way to properly thank you for your help and generosity," said Keir, relinquishing Shakti to Neela before shaking Chacha's hand.

Keir rubbed Shakti's back as she melted onto Neela's shoulder like a rag doll. "Namaste my Shakti. Claire and I will see you soon."

Neela took Shakti inside.

"Don't worry, Dr. Keefe. We understand street children," said Chacha. "We have rescued many over the years, including Neela and Ashook. The gardeners, cooks, teachers, house maids, and laundrymen were either orphaned or abandoned by their biological parents in one way or another. Chachi's grandfather ran a small restaurant on this estate for many years. We expanded so the children could have employment experience as they grew up.

"They are free to leave as they wish but some stay and continue their education and employment here. Some go on to study at universities across the world on scholastic scholarships. We consider each a family member."

Waiting in the doorway, Chachi said, "Indian laws regarding fostering and adoption are strict. Child labor, on the other hand, though officially illegal, is tolerated by corrupt government officials, even encouraged when enough graft is part of the equation. This makes it possible for us to have a house full of happy orphans without constant government supervision. If Claire still wants to adopt Shakti, and that is what Shakti wants as well, we might be able to help with the paperwork. It will however, take a long time, even years."

chapter 17

THE ORPHANAGE

For seven days, I watched the bar of sunlight come through the narrow window and climb the wall. One afternoon, I heard men's voices beyond the door, the only human sound I'd heard since Jamal said goodbye. As the door opened, I tried to stand but I had to bend my neck. My weak legs trembled and I squeezed the bars with my fingers to steady myself. As Keir and Chacha followed the nun into the room, I listened to words I didn't understand, but the intent became clear. They had come to rescue me from this child's prison. The nun opened the cage and Keir carried me out. He hummed as Ashook drove. I remember nothing more until Neela carried me into the washroom.

Gleaming white tiles covered the floor and walls. Neela turned a knob and put her hand in the flow of water coming from near the ceiling. Steam began to fill the room. Neela helped me pull off the dirty dress the nun put on me. As she dropped the dress into the trash and sealed the bag she said, "You will never wear smelly rags ever again, dear Shakti."

I stepped into the flowing hot water and closed my eyes.

Gratitude, more powerful than the water, washed away the stench of the orphanage and the street.

Neela rubbed soap onto a soft cloth and washed week-old dried blood from my face and bald head. The smell of Claire filled the room. "Klaa-r." I said aloud.

"You will see Claire soon. I promise. Now you must rest. You are safe here." Neela spoke Hindi. Cook brought us each a bowl of rice and dahl and we sat on the mat to eat. It was the first time I ate from a bowl. Neela pushed a stool to the sink and showed me how to wash my bowl with liquid soap that smelled like Claire's kitchen.

Neela helped me use a little brush and strange tasting paste from a tube. "This is the toothbrush you will use every day. See, the handle is sunshine-yellow. It is just for you. Mine is bigger and sky-blue." Sometimes Radeeka had found a twig for me to chew to clean my teeth but I had never seen such a brush as this. I tried to mimic Neela. I buried my face in a fluffy dry towel and breathed in the clean smell. It was the first time I brushed my teeth.

We sat on a mat in the bedroom while Neela rocked me in her lap and sang. We slept on the mat together.

The next morning, while Neela slept, I crept to the window wearing the pink nightgown Neela had given me. Golden sunrise appeared on the horizon and glowed over the trees, flowers, and grass. I had seen the horizon only once before, from Claire's flat.

Neela soon joined me at the window. Without talking, we watched a new day dawn.

A new day and my new life.

After a hug, Neela used the western-style toilet and so did I. Neela showed me how to use toilet paper to clean myself. I stood on the little bench to reach the sink and we washed our hands. I rubbed and rubbed, making lots of suds and let the hot water rise it away. It was the first time I washed my hands after making my toilet and the first time I did the needful indoors.

Neela led me to the kitchen. We walked to a big white box. Cold air, filled with the scent of fresh fruits and vegetables erupted from inside. "Always, enough food," said Cook with a kind smile that made me feel safe and welcome.

Neela and I took a walk through the orchard. Neela carried a basket. She put on her sandals and showed me how to put on the ones she presented to me. It was the first time I wore shoes.

We walked and listened to big green birds I learned were parrots. Neela picked a green papaya. I held the big, ripe fruit and inhaled its scent. I didn't know that food grew on trees.

Neela stretched and jumped to capture small green fruit that smelled crisp and peppery. She called it lime.

Sweet smelling yellow fruit hung just out of Neela's reach so she hoisted me onto her shoulders so I could pick the fruit she called mango. I handed each one to her to put into the basket with the lime and papaya.

By the door, we took off our sandals and put them on a low bench with other shoes of all sizes.

My chair was higher than Neela's as we sat at a big round table. I watched Cook scoop slimy black seeds from the papaya and place orange bite-size pieces on small plates. She cut a lime into wedges, squeezed the juice over the papaya, and placed the plates in front of us. I devoured the papaya, then watched Neela chew each bite. It was the first time I sat in a chair at a dining table.

As other residents of Bhojan Thali began to enter the kitchen, Cook placed bigger bowls of food in the middle of the table, and called the name of each dish "upma with coconut chutney, idli with shredded vegetables, dosa, and vada."

The others introduced themselves and welcomed me as they took their places at the table. I watched them fill their plates with as much food as they wanted. As they paused before eating, I breathed the love and felt the gratitude as if it were thick mist rising around the table.

When they finished, each person, child or adult, washed his or her plate in a tub of soapy water then rinsed and placed it in the drying rack. An older boy held me up so I could wash my bowl too.

chapter 18

WAITING

Claire arrived at the office with good intentions but soon realized she couldn't focus on anything but Shakti's rescue. After reading the engineering report three times without the slightest comprehension, she decided to go home to wait. "I'm not feeling well," Claire lied, rubbing her stomach, "I'm going back to my flat. Call if you need me."

Claire paced around her sitting room wondering what Chacha and Keir had encountered at the orphanage. She heated a bowl of tinned soup for lunch. Seven days had passed since the policeman tossed naked little Shakti into that old paddy wagon. Keir had been gone for hours.

A knock at the door startled her. Birdai, the building caretaker, stood smiling at her as five small men ducked under her arm, chattering in Marathi and pointing at the AC unit. They were the AC maintenance crew. They asked, through mime and deduction, if she had a stool or ladder. She didn't, so they stood on her dining room chairs. They pulled the AC filters out and used a noisy industrial strength hair dryer to blow dirt out of the unit in her living room.

She closed the bedroom doors as the living room filled with dust. She began coughing. One bare-footed fellow came through the room with wet, dripping filters, after washing them in the maid's shower.

As they left, the maid arrived to clean the flat as she did every afternoon. At first, Clair thought daily cleaning service was over-indulgent but she soon realized how fast the dust and grime seeped into the apartment. When they'd gone, Claire took a shower, poured herself a glass of wine, and tried to read a book.

At last, she heard Keir climbing the stairs two at a time. He burst in and swept her off her feet with a hug. "She is safe. Shakti is safe. We found her in the orphanage. They shaved her head and she got a little scratched up by that nasty cop but she'll be fine. . . ." He collapsed onto the sofa, put his face in his hands, and wept. Until this moment he thought his concern for Shakti was due to his love for Claire. Now he knew, Shakti has stolen his heart as well.

Claire stood beside him, rubbing his back, waiting for the story.

"There was no sign of Father Adesh and his red eyed monsters. The policeman had literally thrown Shakti into the same cage where that little boy died a few weeks ago." Keir stared at the floor. "It was deplorable. In your country or mine, we wouldn't treat animals with such cruelty. Chacha told me that the nuns and the police believe street children are feral animals that must be tamed." Keir took a deep, halting breath, as if he hadn't taken a breath all day. "Chacha gave the nun a fat envelope and demanded she open Shakti's cage."

Claire leaned on his shoulder, trembling as if her fever had returned.

"Are you all right?" he asked, looking up.

"Yes, I'm fine, but you still haven't told me where Shakti is now."

He patted her hand on his shoulder. "I scooped her up and Ashook drove us to Bhojan Thali—Chacha and Chachi's estate. There are many more buildings we didn't see when we had dinner there. Chachi and Chacha have been taking care of orphans for years, Ashook is one of their graduates."

"Ashook? I thought they were his auntie and uncle."

"That's what he calls them and they consider him family. All the orphans are considered family. It's amazing. The gardeners, the chefs, almost everyone working there was once a street child. It appears that Chacha buys their freedom with the understanding that they will work at Bhojan Thali, and officials look the other way because he donates money."

Claire gasped. "You mean he buys the children like slaves and makes them work?"

"No! The arrangement is with the government, not the children. Once he gets a child out of the orphanage or off the street, he employs cooks, nannies, and teachers to take care of them. They stay only if they want to. Neela, one of their staff members, will be Shakti's nanny and stay with her every minute until she feels safe and grows healthier. "

As Keir recovered his composure, Claire's tears welled, as if she had stayed composed until he could manage her collapse. "I'm so glad she's okay, and with people that will take care of her. Can we see her?" She melted onto the sofa next to him.

"Of course, Auntie invited us to visit as we wish. . . ." Keir sensed that her sorrow encompassed far more than Shakti's ordeal. He held her while heavy sobs racked her body.

"What else is bothering you, Claire?" He squeezed

her shoulders. "I suspect there's more to this than Shakti's safety." After a while, holding her trembling body close, he asked, "Who is Lisa?"

Her head snapped to face him, "What do you know about Lisa?"

"I know nothing. . . except that the nurse told me you called the name. You were delirious with fever after Shakti's capture." He hesitated for a moment then decided to go on, "I've never seen such a violent physical reaction to that kind of trauma, there must be more. . . ."

Claire walked to the refrigerator as if pulling an over-loaded bullock wagon. She poured herself a glass of chardonnay. "Do you want a glass?" she asked, gathering her strength.

"No thanks, I'll have Scotch. Sit, I'll get it myself."

They settled onto the sofa. She began her story in a stiff voice, as if narrating a documentary.

"I told you about my engagement in 1970. . . . In those days, the US government drafted young men to fight in Vietnam. Jim's Conscientious Objector application was denied so he escaped to Canada without me. I never heard from him again. After he left, I realized I was pregnant. He never knew and I never told my parents. I was in an accelerated undergrad program and worked for a professor, grading papers. I didn't tell anyone at the university that I was pregnant. If I had, I couldn't have kept my job. Pregnant women weren't allowed to work at the university until ten years later. I gained a lot of weight and they thought I was just getting fat with the stress of the heavy load and losing my fiancé. No one suspected. I graduated days before Lisa was born.

"I lived on the money my parents deposited into my account for grad school tuition and expenses."

She stared at the wall and shrugged, "That alone is enough to make me dizzy with gratitude in light of Shakti's life. . . ." She struggled to breathe, as if the air thinned with altitude. "When Lisa was about Shakti's age, I started the MBA program. I hired a baby sitter, got a part time job, and took a heavy load so I could finish as fast as possible." She breathed deeply, and took a sip from her quivering wine glass.

"My parents would have been surprised to meet Lisa when they returned from Asia, but one day when I got home from class, Lisa was burning up with fever. The sitter told me she'd been fussy all afternoon but there was no way to reach me. By the time we got to the emergency room, Lisa was convulsing. By morning. . . my little girl was dead." Claire stared at the wall, trembling.

As she talked, Keir sat still as stone looking at the floor, resting his elbows on his knees, not wanting to intrude on the space she needed. He turned to her, "Meningitis?"

She nodded. "When my parents left for Siberia, I was too ashamed to tell them I was pregnant. I remember Mom holding my face in her hands and looking into my eyes. I'm sure she knew. Lisa was born six months later. Occasionally they called, but our conversations were brief because of the bad connection. I wrote austere letters filled with current events, Viet Nam war protests, and political dialog, nothing about my own life. When they came home, Mom knew something terrible had happened but I let her think I was upset about Jim's escape to Canada. I didn't want to disappoint her and I guess she didn't want to intrude. I finished my MBA, and took a job in Boston, as far from the memories as I could get." Claire looked at Keir. Her face twisted with grief, "You're the only person on the planet who knows my story."

Keir understood her pain. He hoped that he and Shakti could help Claire move beyond the wall of grief that kept her emotions hidden.

chapter 19

CLARISSA

In 1950, when Claire was born, her parents, Clarissa and Robert, bought a two-bedroom cottage and an acre of land on the shores of Lake Washington, not far from the University of Washington campus. Its appeal included a carriage house for Claire's nanny. Every room of the little house, including the laundry, had a view of Lake Washington and the Cascade Mountains.

Clarissa, born in 1908, had a hearty disposition and a passion for scientific research. In 1970, as Claire finished her senior year at University of Washington, Clarissa and Robert unearthed a well-preserved grave in Siberia. The corpse had remained frozen for over 10,000 years. Robert believed that a male shaman occupied the grave. He assumed the body, buried with professional accouterments, must be male. He read the past by reference to the present.

He wrote a paper about the mummified medicine man, but Clarissa insisted the grave held a female Etügen Eke. She fought for all women, even their prehistoric bones.

Years later, when DNA tests verified the mummy's

gender, Robert sill would not concede to Clarissa that the mummy was female. He wrote another paper, labeling the mummy a shaman's wife. Clarissa vehemently disagreed. She spent the rest of her life proving that the frozen body could have been a revered female healer in her own right, buried with rattles, drums, feathers, bowls, and pipes, the tools of her own occupation.

Clarissa, Claire and the governess joined Robert on international expeditions whenever they could. When Claire started kindergarten, Clarissa accepted a professorship at the U. For twelve years, until Claire was out of high school, Robert traveled without Clarissa. When he was on location, Claire and her mother joined him during summer breaks and holidays.

Xi'an's terracotta army lured Robert and Clarissa to China in the summer of 1986. Climbing down the bamboo scaffolding into the dig site, Robert slipped. Clarissa stood helpless as his head hit the rock wall on his way to the bottom. A month later, she returned to Seattle with his ashes in an urn.

Claire offered to move back to Seattle to help her mother and live in the carriage house, but Clarissa wouldn't have it. "I'm only 78. I'll let you know if and when I need help."

An ancient Chinese cloisonné urn, half filled with Robert's ashes, remained on the mantel for ten years.

🐘 🐘 🐘

For Clarissa's 88th birthday, Claire took a break from work to visit her mother in Seattle. Before sunrise, they sat by the kitchen window, drinking coffee, enjoying the pre-dawn view of the mountains and water. "Let's sit on the dock and watch the sun come up like we did when I was in elementary school."

"Let's!"

Balancing big mugs of steaming coffee, they briskly walked the rock path to the dock. Both in bathrobes and bare feet, Claire marveled at her vibrant, effervescent 88-year-old mother. She showed no signs of slowing. They sat on the weathered wood, dangling their feet above Lake Washington enjoying stillness unique to early morning on calm water. Golden fingers of light fanned from the horizon ahead of the sun. Claire scooted closer to her mother, leaving no space between them. Clarissa put her thin, sun-leathered arm over Claire's shoulders. Clouds drifted like gold and magenta smoke over Mt. Rainier while the snow-covered Cascade Range glowed like an iridescent coral reef.

"I love sunrise," Claire murmured, stretching to touch the water, creating ripples in the reflected sky.

"Why didn't you tell me about the baby?" Clarissa said in her soft oboe-tones.

"How do you know about Lisa?" Claire was not surprised that her mother knew.

"When we came home I saw the insurance statement for the University Medical Center where you delivered, and the emergency room bill from the night she died. I can't imagine the pain you endured—still endure." She looked at Claire. "I hoped you'd tell me someday, when you were ready."

"It's still difficult to talk about Lisa. As long as no one knew, I didn't have to face the pain again. She was quite precocious. I made tons of photo albums so you could see every stage. I couldn't wait for you to meet her. . . ."

Clarissa's weathered arm tightened around Claire's shoulders, "I love you Claire, but what's more, I respect you. As a little girl you made wise decisions." A memory floated up from forty years before, "Remember the time you tried to raise that orphaned gosling in your bedroom?" She laughed,

"Oh my goodness the smell!"

"The boat I built to sail around the world was a bit of a disaster," Claire laughed.

"Yes, but you were wearing a life jacket when the boat sank. And you knew how to swim back to the dock."

"I'm so sorry Mom. In '71 it was a big deal to have a baby out of wedlock. Now days, no one would notice. I always told you everything. . . but I was so ashamed. . . . If we'd been closer, geographically, I would have come to you for support, but you and Dad were having such fun in Siberia with that frozen mummy. I didn't want to spoil everything and it was impossible to talk on the phone."

Clarissa hugged Claire, "There is nothing you could have done. Meningitis is a horrible disease. . . extremely difficult to diagnose until. . . it's too late. The child's death is not your fault."

"That's what the doctor said." Claire put her head on her Mother's shoulder. "I love you Mom."

They listened to the stillness until a loon's mournful wail eclipsed the silence, as if it knew the future.

Claire and Clarissa planned to have dinner at the Alexis to celebrate Clarissa's birthday, but first, Clarissa spoke to the Women's Anthropological Society regarding the pre-historic female shaman. With passion, Clarissa implored the women in attendance to stand up for truth beyond patriarchy. "As women, we must write the history of all people," she instructed, "not just the history of the men who win wars." She took questions from the audience, and navigated the stairs to her seat like a twenty-something. As the applause subsided, and people stood to leave the auditorium, she collapsed and died on Claire's shoulder.

Claire flew back to Boston, quit her job as VP of Operations at a telecom company, sold her furniture, and moved into her parent's home on Lake Washington. She made no effort to redecorate. The cottage had become a museum, filled with books, baskets, blankets, rugs, and pottery from her parent's adventures in Kashmir, Mongolia, England, Siberia, and beyond. Framed photographs spoke to her: father standing in a beam of sunlight deep in an excavation pit, waving up at the camera, both parents posing near a collection of ancient bits of pottery, mother at a market holding a basket of fresh produce with baby Claire secured to her back with a length of colorful handwoven fabric. Their collection, imbued with energetic vibration, created a lively atmosphere full of history, as if projecting holographic movies from every shelf, every wall, creating tangible memories of her parents lives.

She spent months sorting through Clarissa and Robert's estate, and meeting with their attorney and CPA. She discovered that they had purchased property during each expedition. When they moved on, they rented the house to a member of the local team or a professor. Claire now owned property all over the world. Fortunately, her mother's accountant was an honest woman who had kept meticulous records of every purchase, expense, and rental payment.

Carrying the cloisonné urn holding their ashes, Claire traced her parent's adventures, from Siberia, to Crete, to Spain, to Mongolia, leaving a sprinkle of ash in each location. She spent time getting to know their former colleagues although many of them were quite old. She made decisions about each property, deciding to keep a beautiful cottage in Crete and a white stucco villa in Spain. She donated the remaining properties to the universities where her parents had studied and lectured.

🐘 🐘 🐘

Not long after she returned to Seattle, a recruiter called. "My condolences on the loss of your mother."

She said, "Thank you," but her tone clearly communicated, *what do you really want?*

"You have a reputation in the telecom industry, Ms. Kaine," he reported. "My client company needs a telecom executive with international experience. Your background is perfect."

"I have no interest in an opportunity in India or anywhere else. I have just returned from a year-long trip spreading my parent's ashes."

The recruiter was exceptionally persuasive. "What would it take for you to consider this assignment?" he asked after outlining the major aspects of the job.

She began to consider the idea of helping to bring Internet, cellular phone service, and jobs to India. *It could be an incredible opportunity,* she thought. She gave him a figure she considered outrageous, more than triple her salary in Boston. Without hesitation he agreed. "The compensation package will also include lodging, health care, stock options in the client company, and a per diem for expenses. If you agree, I'll arrange a meeting. The company is there in Seattle."

She couldn't refuse.

chapter 20

MR. HAMADANI

"Husband! Where are you? Where is Radeeka?"

On the day Raj and Ruchi died in the accident, Mr. Hamadani called his wife from a pay phone. "The dear child overheard the policeman's report of the accident. He told me he would be taking her to the orphanage. Before I could tell Radeeka we would take care of her, she dashed away. I couldn't catch her." Mr. Hamadani sounded like an old man with a shaking raspy voice.

After hanging up, he continued searching until well after dark, and took a taxi home.

At the Kodak shop the next day he made copies of a picture he had taken of Radeeka. She grinned at the camera with a clean happy face. She wore her favorite yellow-kitty t-shirt. A barrette with three daises held her ponytail. The same favorite outfit she wore the morning she learned she was an orphan.

Mr. Hamadani hired a replacement doorman and left the apartment building before dawn each morning, searching farther and farther from the apartment building. A bread walla recognized the photo but it had been weeks since Radeeka bought a roll from his cart. "I am remembering that girl," he stabbed a finger at the image, "too fresh for being a beggar child." The clerk in the sari shop also recognized the photo but had no idea which way the child had gone. Sometimes Mr. Hamadani rode the bus watching intently. One day he thought he saw her with a group of younger children. He got off of the bus, crossed traffic, and faced the girl. "Radeeka, is that you?" he took her by the shoulders. "I am so sorry to frighten you, I am looking for Radeeka," he said as he released her.

He checked in dark rat infested alleys and behind rancid dumpsters. He walked for hours every day, wearing traditional *kurtas* and brown leather sandals. He had no way to know whether she went north, south or east in the huge city. His back ached and his legs and feet throbbed.

One afternoon he rested on a bench, with his face in his hands, elbows on his knees, catching his breath, trying not to sob. Just as he stood, a bus passed close to the curb and the rear-view mirror struck his head. He awoke a week later in hospital with a nurse tending to the gash on his head. Mrs. Hamadani was at his bedside.

"Has Radeeka come home?" he croaked, squeezing his wife's hand, looking into a face, blurred by his head trauma.

"No dear husband, she has not come back."

He went home after two weeks in hospital, but it took several more weeks for Mr. Hamadani's vision to clear and headaches to subside. When he was well enough, he resumed his search. He carried copies of Radeeka's picture and gave it to anyone who might see her.

Months later, after the raid at the hotel fountain, Radeeka walked the streets alone mumbling to herself. *I knew we shouldn't go back to the hotel so often. It's my fault Shakti and Jamal were arrested.* She vowed to listen to the voice her papa had called intuition.

Shakti is young and not a thief, so the police will take her to the orphanage, she thought. Jamal has gone to jail, she had no doubt. She worried what awful things were happening to them. Looking down at her dirty toes extending over the soles of her outgrown sandals, jostled by the crowd, she ran smack into a man on the sidewalk. He grabbed her by the shoulders. She struggled, but he held firm.

"Radeeka, is that you?"

This time Mr. Hamadani knew he had found Radeeka. He saw her father's eyes in the dirty, hollow face.

"How do you know my name?" she wailed, struggling like a rabbit caught in a snare.

He knelt in front of her and forced her to look into his face. "Radeeka, it's me, Atif Hamadani," his voice loud but calm. "Radeeka. Don't you remember me? The doorman? I've been searching for you all these months."

"Please don't take me to the orphanage, please," she cried. Afraid to believe her inner voice, she didn't know whether to hug him or flee.

"You poor sweet child. You will not be going to the orphanage. Hear me! You are not going there." He looked into her eyes. "Listen to me. The flat belongs to you. The entire building belongs to you. Your father left a trust in your name so that you would have all you needed if such a terrible thing should happen. You ran away before I could tell you, my wife and I are your legal guardians. We love you like our own daughter. You must come home with me now."

Her struggle stilled. She stood motionless with a vacuous stare, then collapsed into Mr. Hamadani's arms like a kite that lost the wind.

She awoke on her parent's bed, as if the past year had been a garish nightmare.

Mrs. Hamadani was patting her hand. "Are you feeling better, Radeeka my sweet?"

Radeeka looked into the woman's familiar eyes, "I want mama and papa."

Mrs. Hamadani hummed a lullaby as grief forced open the stoic levee that had held Radeeka's tears all that time. She hugged the child close. Her own eyes teared with grief and relief, and from the odor that filled the room. She helped Radeeka into the bathroom and turned on the shower. Radeeka stepped out of her sepia-colored jeans and pulled off her t-shirt, the yellow kitten invisible beneath the filth that had been her life.

"I will put these in the trash," said Mrs. Hamadani.

"No! Wait!" shrieked Radeeka. Like swimming through syrup, fumbling with the dirty jeans, she found the silver barrette in a pocket. "This belongs to Shakti." She clutched the barrette, struggling to release it into Mrs. Hamadani's palm, as if letting go of the barrette also let go of Shakti. In a fog of churning memories, she remembered the morning Shakti joined her on the street; Shakti's clear, chocolate-milk skin, the depth of her honey-gold eyes. In slow motion, she felt the fountain's cool water, saw the policeman, his arm around naked Shakti, and she heard the slap of her own feet on the sidewalk as she ran from the fountain.

Radeeka was home, her parents were dead, but she hadn't grasped the enormity. She had aged a lifetime but she was still a nine-year-old child. She worried about her street family, feeling responsible for their lives.

With Mrs. Hamadani's help, Radeeka stepped under the flowing hot water. She tilted her head back. The water began to rinse away the smell but could not dislodge the grief.

Mrs. Hamadani poured shampoo onto Radeeka's head.

As if submerged, Radeeka heard Mrs. Hamadani's muffled voice "These mats are impossible to comb out, we need to cut your hair." She heard the scissors strain through the mats, and shivered as cold steal touched her scalp. As her matted locks dropped into the waste bin, Radeeka's mind flashed back to the first time she stood in a shower.

Mama adjusted the water temperature and gave me a washcloth that smelled of soap. As Mama's fingers massaged shampoo into my hair, she told me, "Radeeka, you can shampoo your own hair now." I felt so grown up, but after playing with the suds and rinsing it from my hair, Mama wrapped me like a baby in a soft sweet-smelling towel and as she so often did, covered my clean face with kisses.

chapter 21

HONG KONG

The Indian government required that expats leave the country every ninety days to renew work visas, so Claire arranged meetings with equipment vendors in Hong Kong. It was much easier to leave Mumbai knowing that Shakti was off the streets. For a week, Claire enjoyed a luxurious suite at the Grand Hyatt in Wan Chai with a view of Hong Kong Harbor.

Between meetings, she took time to contact her attorney in Seattle and began the process of establishing the Clarissa C. Kaine Endowment Fund to help educate orphans.

She flew Cathay Pacific business class back to Mumbai. An amenity kit waited on her window seat. Settling in, enjoying the extra space of an empty seat next to her, she took off her shoes and unwrapped the amenity kit. She found a sleeping mask, heavy socks, and toiletries provided for passenger comfort during the international flight. She pulled on the flight booties, put the sleeping mask on the seat next to her, zipped the bag, and stowed it in the pocket in front of her. The flight attendant served champagne and gave her the choice of a veg or non-veg meal.

Claire savored the attractively presented roasted chicken, potatoes, and steamed vegetables as if it would be her last meal. Pulling the sleeping mask over her eyes, she put her seat back but two glasses of champagne, and a good meal couldn't help her relax. Her mind raced.

She contemplated social change in India compared to the US. There was no caste system per se in the US, but the similarities were obvious. Affluent males dominated government in both countries. In the US, slaves were emancipated in 1865 and women were given the right to vote in 1920 but it took until 1964 for The Civil Rights Act to outlaw discrimination based on race, color, religion, sex, or national origin. Now, in 1997, discrimination was still a way of life in the US.

In India, the caste system became illegal in 1947, but still marked professional divisions locked into place by birth and a rigid structure of social mores.

Giving up on sleep, she used the clean toilet and on the way back to her seat, took a copy of the Maharashtra Times offered by the flight attendant. She noticed that journalists used politically correct language to report on social hierarchy, wealth, politics, and the powerful influencers like actors and cricket stars, but she knew that the unmentioned caste system still dictated reality in the daily lives of most of India's population. She'd seen it firsthand, from the *Brahmin* executives to *Shudra* construction staff in the office and hotel. The hierarchy was not as obvious to her in India as in the US, where disproportionate housekeeping and janitorial jobs were still held by people of color.

Claire read yet another article about a "kitchen accident." The wife had died leaving two young daughters. Claire knew that the husband would expect to collect a dowry from a new wife who would, hopefully, produce a son. Kitchen fires were reported regularly but the reports never implied guilt or motive.

Claire hoped building the telecommunications systems would help establish new jobs, and educational opportunities in an improved economy, even for the poor, but she knew that change came slowly on both sides of the planet.

chapter 22

BHOJAN THALI

*M*orning sun cast shadows on the lawn as the gates parted.

"How beautiful!" said Claire. "This place looks so much bigger in bright sunlight. Look at the gardens!"

"They grow a lot of their own food here," said Keir. "I wonder if Shakti had any idea where food came from, beyond the dumpsters."

"I've been thinking about what it would be like to be Shakti this past week. Think of the new experiences she's having," she said.

"All the fresh food she can eat, clean water to drink, feeling safe, taking a bath, clean clothes... makes me mindful of the abundance in my own life. . . ." said Keir.

When they arrived at the house, Keir noticed Ashook's grin when Neela stepped into the portico with Shakti. Keir nudged Claire with his elbow, nodded his head toward Ashook, "Looks like Ashook and Neela are especially fond of each other," but Claire only had eyes for Shakti, hardly noticing how different she looked without her matted hair.

She sprang from the car and knelt in front of the little girl, "Hello Shakti."

To her surprise, Shakti replied, "Hal-low Klaa-r."

Neela smiled down at them, "We practiced all week."

Shakti hugged Claire and put her head on Claire's shoulder.

She looked up at Keir standing behind them. "Tank oo Keeer."

Keir scooped her away from Claire and swung around. "It's so good to see you Shakti. You look splendid! I love you to bits!" He kissed her bald head.

"Until she found Claire, Shakti never knew that strangers could be so kind and generous, or that she might visit a world beyond her life on the street," said Neela. "She is aware that you saved her from that awful cage the policeman threw her into."

"Good morning Claire, Keir," said Chachi. Shakti took Chachi's outstretched hand and they all went inside, except for Ashook and Neela. Keir saw a yellow glow of love between them as they walked across the lawn toward the mango trees.

"I see that Ashook and Neela are fond of each other," said Keir.

"Yes," said Chachi. "They have been special friends since they were children. We will be having a love marriage one day soon."

"How is a love marriage different from any other marriage?"

"Ashook and Neela fell in love and chose to marry, unlike many marriages in India that are arranged."

"Aren't they too young?" asked Keir.

"Neela is twenty-three. When she was just a few weeks old, she was in a car crash with her family on the Pune-

Mumbai highway," Chachi told them. "She was thrown from the car and landed in soft mud and cow dung. Her mother and father were killed. Her uncle, who worked for Chacha, was her only living relative but he didn't want the girl. Neela is the first child we brought home to live with us as our own. In fact she is still the only child we legally adopted.

"Ashook is about the same age but we don't know his exact birthday," she told them. "He remembers the airport construction when he was living in the Dharavi slum with his family. It had been an unusually wet monsoon season and mosquitoes tortured them day and night until Dengue fever overwhelmed the slum. At first Ashook's family experienced nausea, fever, and headaches but they all seemed to recover. About a week later, as is common with Dengue, his family members began bleeding from the eyes and vomiting blood. Within a few days, only Ashook survived. He must have been about four years old. He wandered Mumbai, eating from the hotel garbage bins but returned to Dharavi to sleep.

"I knew one of the women his mother cleaned house for. When she told me of the family's misfortune, Chacha and his driver searched Dharavi for days. They found him and brought him to Bhojan Thali.

"Neela and Ashook have both been studying for college entrance exams. He hopes to become a surgeon and she wants to be a pediatrician. Their dream is to start their family in America, then return to India."

"I had no idea he wanted to go into medicine," said Keir. "How did I miss that? He's been my driver for four years."

"Ashook is a professional chauffeur. He would never presume to discuss his personal life with his client. You may have seen the big satchel of books on the front seat of the car. When he isn't driving, he studies."

"I hardly think of him as an employee!"

Shakti stood patiently, holding Chachi's hand, keen to show Claire and Keir her new world.

Chachi led them upstairs to a large light-filled room with books, blocks, easels, crayons, dolls, trucks and child-size as well as adult-size tables and chairs. "This is amazing!" said Claire. "It is looks like the University of Washington's Montessori classroom."

Children ages four to sixteen milled about, sitting at tables or squatting on the floor, reading books, building with blocks, or painting at the easels. The older children helped the younger ones. A boy sorted a box of sea shells, using a big reference book, focused on identifying each shell. In the corner, a girl huddled over a fourteen inch CRT computer monitor, while another slid a floppy disk into the drive.

Shakti let go of Chachi's hand and walked across the marble floor to the library corner.

"It is difficult to comprehend the scope of Shakti's learning already," Chachi went on. "She had never taken a shower until she met you, Claire. She still hasn't combed her own hair but she will learn as it grows. She remains more comfortable sleeping on the floor. She never knew if or when she would eat. We've been careful to add new foods to her diet gradually, until the dysentery is healed."

Shakti selected a copy of *Good Night Moon*, squatted on the rug next to the shelf, and opened the book in front of her. She hugged her legs, rested her chin on her knees, and turned the pages as if delicate dried leaves held the words. The pictures of rooms, rabbits, and furniture fascinated her.

Claire sat down on a little chair and Shakti brought the book to her. Shakti stood with her arm on Claire's shoulder as Claire read aloud. Claire tried to imagine what the illustrations meant to Shakti. A simple story like *Good Night Moon* must seem like Harry Potter riding a broom, she thought.

"I assume Shakti's had a physician's attention," Keir said to Chachi.

"Yes, of course. Dr. Chopra visits us once a month or more if we are needing him. He brought medicine for her dysentery and a special salve to heal the infected rat bites on her arms, legs, and ears. She is in surprisingly good health. And…," she gave Keir's a knowing smile, "I have studied energy healing. I do what I can to help all of the children."

"I did what I could while she was in the car that night. She soaked up my energy like a dry sponge." Keir's voice softened. "You're doing it now."

As Claire read to Shakti, she didn't see the green light arch as Chachi focused her considerable healing power onto Shakti.

"Yes, I send my healing energy to help her adjust to being here, to heal the physical wounds, but I think she would thrive in any environment. Shakti has spent her life in the present moment. She does not fear the unknown, and her detachment to outcome is remarkable. I have spent hours observing her behavior, both alone and with the other children. She is extraordinarily self-actualized, fulfilled by her own thoughts. She is independent, spontaneous and accepts her new world with openness and curiosity. She is as non-judgmental as any human I've ever met. We have a special opportunity," she said.

"How so?"

"Dr. Keefe, do you meditate?" asked Chachi.

"Yes, I have a twice daily practice."

"Have you ever tried to find stillness, that place where you are one with the Universe?"

"Yes, of course. Life's chatter creeps into every meditation," he said, "monkey mind," waving his hands around his head.

"Shakti told Neela that one of her street-mates, Radeeka, taught her to meditate every morning and evening and she continues the practice. I suspect she hears no mind chatter. No thought disrupts her meditation. Her stillness is absolute. We must not interfere."

Keir watched Claire read to Shakti and saw the beautiful arch of light shining between them. His smile became a grin and he shook his head in disbelief. "Do you see the light between them?"

Chachi nodded.

He went on, "I've seen energy and emotion as colorful light since I was a little boy but never admitted to anyone until now. I understand why the children feel safe with you."

"I am honored that you chose this moment to admit your gift aloud," she said.

They watched Claire and Shakti.

"The energy isn't just between them, it's flowing from Shakti to Claire. Is Shakti helping Claire heal?" he asked.

"I'm pleased you see it too," said Chachi.

Claire glimpsed at them with satisfaction and returned to reading. She had no cognitive awareness of the energy flow, but her body gratefully absorbed every particle.

Chachi and Keir walked toward the easels on the other side of the room. "Claire grew up with loving parents and all she needed in terms of nourishment and educational opportunities, but she. . ." Keir paused to find the right words.

"It is obvious that Claire is a powerful and competent business woman, but I doubt that her professional persona serves who she really is inside, and. . . I can see that she has suffered a great a trauma in the past and lives behind a wall of self-preservation."

"Do you think Shakti can help her?" he said. He knew the answer.

"I know it. What's more, I believe it is Shakti's calling to help us all."

"You mean the human race."

She nodded. "Shakti was born knowing that universal love has no opposite. . . ." Chachi paused. "To Shakti, love is like breathing; it's how she lives. Our responsibility, as her care givers, is to support her needs and keep her healthy without restricting her gifts. I hope Claire understands."

"I will help her understand," his voice deepened with love and warmth. He watched Claire unfold from the little chair, "I hope we have the opportunity to discuss energy healing again sometime soon," he said quietly as Claire walked toward them.

Claire took Chachi's hand in hers. Their fingers aligned like piano keys, tears of gratitude hung on Claire's long blond lashes, "How do we thank you?"

"Shakti's smile is all the thanks I need," said Chachi, thinking, *Now Shakti will focus on her calling. . . like a young sage who has found her ashram.*

chapter 23

BHOJAN THALI SCHOOL

Soon I was spending each day in the school room. At first, I stood at the sand table with two children my age but they were much taller. While Neela helped a girl read a book, I watched the older children move around the room. One sat at the computer, others built with blocks. A small group sat around a teacher leaning to write numbers and letters.

The next day I sat at a child-size table, still watching the others while I made drawings with fat crayons in all colors. I drew a big circle with little lines all around. The next day I gave my circles arms and legs and put eyes and a mouth in each circle. As the week progressed I did nothing but draw. I drew blue sky and white clouds with green grass all across the paper. I drew green trees with big yellow fruit hanging low to the ground. I drew brown tree trunks and limbs with spiky green fruit that looked like mammoth burrs. I drew the garden with rows of green on brown dirt. I drew black water-buffalo like the ones I'd seen on the street, and oxen with big humps pulling men on carts. As I finished each piece, Neela, Chachi, *or another teacher hung it on a wire with clothes pins.*

One morning, instead of drawing, I became interested in a book I found in the library corner, Good Night Moon.

Chachi sat down with me and began to read. She pointed at the pictures and offered a word for each object and a voice for the letters.

The more I looked, the more things I saw. A blue rabbit sat in a yellow rocking chair knitting a green sweater. A smaller rabbit covered with a green blanket slept in a bed, all in a room with a fireplace, a red balloon, and a telephone. I had so many questions, "What is sweater? What is rabbit? Why does chair have curved feet? What is knitting? What is telephone? What is moon?"

That night, while the other children slept, Neela took me into the yard for a special surprise. We lay on a blanket watching stars brighter than I had ever seen. Soon, the full moon rose like a street light silhouetting the mango tree.

I fell asleep as the moon climbed above us. It was the first time I saw the full moon. We repeated our adventure on many nights so I could see all of its phases.

chapter 24

Finding Radeeka

"Could she be the same child?" Keir said to himself as they left the estate. "Radeeka. . . ?"

"What are you talking about?" asked Claire. "Who's Radeeka?"

"Shakti has mentioned her on several occasions. . . Shakti had a child-sized surrogate mother when I first saw them on the street. While you were reading to Shakti, Chachi mentioned that Radeeka taught Shakti to meditate. I got a strange feeling. A colleague of mine, Dr. Raj Khawaja and his wife were killed in a car accident just after the Ganesh Festival last year. He loved having a beautiful little girl and he was a wonderful father. He taught her to speak English, Hindi, and Marathi. And, he taught her to meditate twice a day. Mr. Hamadani gave me a photo of her. . . , but I had forgotten." He fumbled with his wallet. "He told me she ran away when she heard the policeman tell Mr. Hamadani that she would be taken to the orphanage."

He found the photo tucked among credit cards and IDs. Radeeka grinned at the lens, her full face sparkling with happiness. He could see the resemblance to her papa. Holding the photo so Claire could see, he said, "It's difficult to believe that the scrawny child with matted hair and filthy clothing is the same little girl."

"You mean the one who held Shakti's hand at the fountain?"

"Yes, I wonder if that little girl is Raj's daughter."

"How do we find her? If Radeeka thinks she'll be sent to the orphanage. . ."

Keir scooted to the edge of the car seat, "Ashook, can you take us to Chowpatty Beach, please? I must talk with Mr. Hamadani."

🐘 🐘 🐘

Keir and Claire walked into the lobby of the building once owned by his friend Dr. Raj Khawaja. "Hello, I'm Dr. Keir Keefe. I was a colleague of Dr. Khawaja's."

The doorman extended his hand "Hello, I am Atif Hamadani. Ah, yes, I remember you Dr. Keefe. You came to the memorial service. It was a tragic loss."

"Have you found their daughter?"

The skin around his eyes pinched into deep wrinkles, "Oh yes sir. For over a year, I was walking the streets, looking for her. A week ago, I ran straight into Radeeka not far from your hotel. It took all my strength to hold onto her until I could convince her she was not going to the orphanage. My wife is with her now. Radeeka hasn't left her flat since she came home. My wife and I stay with her, as her parents wished. We have always loved her like our own."

"Claire and I. . . oh, excuse me, Mr. Hamadani, this is Claire Kaine. We watched a group of children beg near the hotel. We often gave them food. . . Now I believe

Radeeka might have been one of them. I am so sorry I didn't recognize her sooner." He held Radeeka's photo. "Radeeka was like a mother to a three-year-old girl, Shakti. I hate to think what would have become of Shakti if not for Radeeka. When the police came last week, Radeeka ran but her little friend Shakti was captured and thrown into the orphanage." Keir gave his account hastily, as if to shorten the children's suffering. "We managed to rescue Shakti with the help of loving and generous people. They have a beautiful estate on the outskirts of Mumbai where they care for and educate orphans."

"It is good to know there are such people in Mumbai," said Mr. Hamadani.

"I can't imagine the trauma poor Radeeka has been through," said Claire. "When they're both ready, do you suppose we could all have a picnic and fly kites on the beach together? I'm certain the girls would love to see each other again."

"That would be splendid, however, Radeeka must feel safe before we can make such a plan. She has not been outdoors since I found her last week," he said. "Her mama and papa have been gone for over a year, but she has just begun to mourn the loss."

"If you think it's appropriate, will you please let Radeeka know we were here? Tell her that Shakti is not at the orphanage. She is safe, well fed, and living with a loving family." Claire gave Mr. Hamadani her card. "Shakti has not ventured beyond the gates of her new home either, but I know she misses Radeeka. They have a bond I can't begin to comprehend."

"Radeeka has mentioned Shakti, and has been worrying about the child. Imagine taking on such responsibility at her age. . . ," he shook his head, "like

her mother, I suppose. Ruchi would be so proud. . . ," he
turned away, still shaking his head. "Knowing Shakti is not
a prisoner at the orphanage, will help Radeeka adjust to
being home."

chapter 25

KEIR AND CHACHI

Every Saturday morning, after dropping Claire at the office, and sometimes during the week if he could get away later in the day, Keir visited Bhojan Thali. Meanwhile, Claire immersed herself in preparing to launch the telecommunications network. Keir gave Claire a complete report on Shakti's progress after each visit.

One morning Keir listened to Shakti read her favorite book, *Good Night Moon,* in both Hindi and English. After only a few months at Bhojan Thali, she was learning to read as well as translate. They walked the estate together while Shakti identified every fruit and vegetable, using both Hindi and English. "We eat breakfast, lunch and dinner," she said. "Food grows here." Keir marveled at how fast she had learned to speak English.

Back inside, Shakti joined other children in a reading class. She was not yet five years old, and much smaller than the other children, but she had already mastered both the Hindi and English alphabet.

Chachi invited Keir to lunch with her on a screened porch near the kitchen.

"I'm glad we have this time to continue our discussion and perhaps to discuss Shakti's progress, her future." With a dark-eyed, piercing gaze, she added, "I'm certain you are understanding how special she is."

"I wish I understood better than I do. She has learned to read but there's more to it. It's difficult to articulate. She is a bright, and agreeable child but, as we discussed before, I know there's more than I fully grasp."

"Shakti has a higher energy vibration than most children her age. I sensed it before I met her," said Chachi.

"What do you mean?"

"Many times, Ashook has identified abandoned children who need rescue, but when he mentioned that you needed help at the orphanage, I felt a sweep of euphoria, as if we were rescuing the planet. . . ." Chachi thought for a moment. "Like ripples in a pond of recovery, each person Shakti helps will help others. And I'm certain her calling is to help others heal."

"I recognized that she was special the first day I saw her turquoise aura with yellow bolts like lightning glowing around her. Most of the people living on the street had almost no light in comparison. Her energy was powerful. I know Claire feels it but she's not cognitively aware yet. As you and I discussed last time we met, Claire doesn't understand that Shakti can help her as much or maybe more than she can help Shakti," he said.

"Claire has a path of awakening ahead of her. Shakti knows no other way to live. As the two of them spend more time together, Claire will become aware of Shakti's energy more cognitively. As Shakti's English improves, she will communicate with Claire at Claire's level," she said.

"Claire's job is taking more and more time and energy. Spending time with Shakti is difficult," said Keir.

"And yet Claire wants to adopt the child?" said Chachi, approaching the true reason for their meeting.

"Claire's job is demanding but it's a short term assignment. Once they launch the network, the company will be run by the Indian partners."

"And Claire will return to Seattle," she said. It was not a question.

"When she arrived, she planned to repatriate at the end of the assignment, yes, but now, she's hoping to stay in Mumbai to be near Shakti." Keir took a sip of ginger pepper tea.

"That's wonderful to hear, Shakti will be pleased."

"Me too!" He raised his brows above the twinkle in his green eyes. "The foundation of their friendship is complex and their bond is powerful. I'm sure Claire senses Shakti's energy and somehow understands that Shakti can help her recover from. . ." He stopped, not wanting to break Claire's confidence.

"I sense Claire's deep grief and misdirected guilt. . . ."
Keir nodded.

"Shakti's life was blessed with spiritual abundance, even when she was hungry on the street." Chachi paused. "Shakti is aware of nothing *but* her authentic Self. No one ever taught Shakti otherwise. Claire on the other hand, has lived with abundance in terms of financial security. She is well educated, and her parents loved her but she is starving spiritually. That is to be expected. Like most Western women, she's living the life she thinks she should live, in this case, as a high powered executive female. I can see she is just beginning the struggle to become her authentic Self. I believe, given the opportunity, Shakti will help Claire grow beyond the pain of her past."

Chachi stood, "Come, I want to show you Shakti's art."

Children's drawings hung on a line in the wide hallway like a row of petroglyphs on a cave wall. It appeared that progressively older children had done the drawings.

"Which one is Shakti's," he asked.

"All of them. She's been a very prolific little artist. Do you see a pattern?"

"From one stage to the next. . . it's like a text book study of a child's motor skill development in terms of art and drawing, from large motor to small motor. . . , amazing. In most children you'd see this kind of progress over a period of a few years."

As he stood back to look up and down the wall he noticed that she had also practiced printing the alphabet. "Her penmanship is improving. . ."

"Something more. . . "

"Each time, the colors are the same for every letter of the alphabet. Do you have that many paint colors?" he asked.

"No, she mixed the paint colors herself. Look at the plastic letters on the magnetic board," she pointed. "Shakti painted each plastic letter to match what she practiced. What's more remarkable, she is also learning the Sanskrit alphabet. There are 46 letters and she has matched the sounds to the colors of the Roman alphabet."

"Synesthesia. . . ," he whispered.

"You have studied synesthesia?"

"I studied brain abnormalities as an undergrad. Some researchers believe that all children are born with synesthesia but as the brain grows, the extra sensory connections unhook. It's so rare there haven't been a lot of studies. Synesthetes, like Stevie Wonder, Leonard Bernstein and possibly Beethoven saw musical notes as colors." He grinned at Chachi, "I can't wait to see what will happen when she learns to read music!" He paused. "I've often wondered if the auras I see myself are caused by my brain connecting emotions with colors."

"Seeing auras could be a form of synesthesia," she said. "I never considered that possibility. There is so much science doesn't know about the brain."

"You mentioned before, you are an energy healer. . . ?" he said in a quiet voice, "I'd like to know more if I could."

"I don't know if my gifts would be diagnosed as synesthesia, but I can *sense* a patient's discomfort and like a convex lens concentrating the sun's rays, I have the ability to focus energy to heal wounds and disease. I cannot intervene however, unless I am asked to do so. . ." Chachi sipped her tea. "Shakti's healing power and natural understanding far exceed my own gifts. I think she might be a medical intuitive."

"You mean she can see an ailment a doctor must test for, or fail to discover at all?"

Chachi nodded. "I'm not certain if she *sees* an ailment or if she just senses it in some way, maybe like I do, but she is too young and inexperienced to discuss her gift with us, or to suggest a course of treatment for an inflicted patient. I have seen her interact with children who are suffering from various ailments as a result of their time on the street. Her empathy is comprehensive. One day a boy skinned his knee while playing soccer. I saw Shakti rub her own knee as if she felt it too. She walked across the field and put her hand on his injury. He recovered quickly."

"I suspect there is a scientific explanation for this phenomenon, similar to synesthesia, where her body mirror's the sensations of others. If she does perceive the pain of others, and the sensations are strong, the condition could be debilitating." he said.

"I have watched closely and so has Neela," said Chachi. "So far, that's the only incident we've seen where Shakti responded in such a way. I suspect the sensations are not painful or distracting to her. Time will tell."

chapter 26

TOGETHER AGAIN

Shakti stood by Ashook's car in the portico, ready to picnic and fly kites at Chowpatty beach. For this occasion, Claire allowed herself a Saturday away from the office.

Keir and Claire had suggested a drive in the car several times before but this was the first time Shakti had agreed, and only if Neela came along.

On the day of her capture, during the trip from the fountain to the orphanage, Shakti saw nothing beyond the dark interior walls of the truck. During her second motor vehicle ride from the orphanage to the Bhojan Thali, she kept her face buried on Keir's shoulder.

Neela sat in the front while Ashook opened the back door. Shakti scooted onto the seat between Keir and Claire. As they passed the gate, Shakti moved onto Keir's lap. He opened the window and like a happy Labrador puppy, Shakti watched the world go by.

Keir had contacted Mr. Hamadani. "Claire and I are picnicking with Shakti on Chowpatty Beach tomorrow.

Do you think the girls could see each other again?"

Mr. Hamadani spoke faster than usual, "My wife and Radeeka have been walking the beach at lunch time every day. Radeeka will not be suspecting. Oh what a lovely surprise it will be."

"Splendid," said Keir. "We'll let the girls discover one another."

🐘 🐘 🐘

As always, Radeeka bowed to Ganesh before leaving the flat and said a little prayer to her mama.

"Let's take the kite with us today," suggested Mrs. Hamadani. They rode the elevator down and waved to Mr. Hamadani as they went through the lobby. A white Mercedes drove past while they waited on the curb for the light to change. Radeeka didn't recognize the short haired girl looking out the open window but she watched the car turn into the parking lot. Her stomach bubbled with excitement but she didn't know why.

Radeeka and Mrs. Hamadani walked to a park bench. Still reluctant to fly her kite without her papa, Radeeka toyed with the kite string bobbin while she watched people getting out of the white car. She recognized the blonde woman wearing western clothes and the tall red haired man who unfolded from other side. They were the foreigners who had offered food by the hotel fountain. A little girl clung to the man. He reached back in to get his hat while the little girl hugged his neck. Radeeka watched them walk to the shore. The warm breeze tossed the girl's short hair as the red haired man knelt to help her take off her sandals. She wiggled her feet in the sand at the edge of the sea. When he released a marigold colored kite into the wind, its white tail twisted as it flew higher. *Could it be?* thought Radeeka.

Shakti's hair, shaved off by the nuns, had grown into a soft black cap. Shorts and a blue blouse replaced her smelly red dress. The rat bites had healed leaving her chocolate milk skin soft and lovely. She had grown two inches and gained weight in the past year. Her once hollow face was now round and healthy and her honey-colored eyes were happy as always.

Shakti walked barefoot in warm beach sand, felt warm salt air on her face and the tug of a kite string in her hand.

She also felt a tug on her heart. She knew instantly who sat on the park bench. Keir captured the kite string just as Shakti let go.

Radeeka had also grown in the year since the police raid. The snarled mats were gone and her short hair was black and silky. She looked older, more like a grown-up.

While Ashook, Neela, Keir, and Claire watched, the two girls walked deliberately toward each other, and stopped, face to face.

Mrs. Hamadani put one hand over her mouth and the other on her heart.

After a long hug, they grasped each other's hands, leaned back, and released sheets of laughter toward the blue sky, spinning like dancers in the sand. Their laughter brought tears to everyone watching, including Mr. Hamadani who had left his post to watch the girls meet again.

chapter 27

PHOTOGRAPHS

"Doctor Keefe, Neela and I are getting married and going to university in America so I will not be driving you any longer. Sunil is a most excellent driver. He has much experience driving Uncle for three years."

"Congratulations Ashook, when is the wedding?"

"In three weeks' time, sir," said Ashook.

"Nice to meet you Sunil," said Keir, shaking Sunil's hand.

"I will be having the same schedule Ashook has been having. Please ring the front desk and I will be driving you," said Sunil. "

"Can you find the camera shop on Kurla Road? I'm buying a surprise for Claire."

While Sunil skillfully pulled the Mercedes into traffic, Ashook sat in the passenger seat. Keir asked Ashook, "What University will you be attending?"

"We are both accepted at the University of Washington in Seattle."

Keir plugged in the charger for the new Nikon SLR camera he'd bought for Claire. He did the same for his own camera.

Inside his camera bag he found a roll of undeveloped film. After the Ganesh Festival, he had put the bag in the closet and forgot to have the roll developed.

Again, he met Sunil and Ashook in the lobby. He asked Sunil to return to the photo shop. "Please wait while the film is developed. Pick up Claire at her office at 6:00 pm. I'll be waiting here in the lobby."

"Yes, of course, sir," said Sunil.

Keir shot the film during the Ganesh Festival over two years before. He'd captured his students drenched by monsoon rain and covered with crimson chandan powder, used to anoint Lord Ganesh as well as bystanders. He'd taken photos of the elaborately crafted and decorated statutes of Lord Ganesh on podiums and trailers pulled by decorated ox carts, painted elephants, and auto rickshaws covered with marigold garlands.

Raj had invited Keir to their flat where, from the tenth floor high above the mob of devotees, they watched the colorful parade of Ganesh statues arriving at Chowpatty Beach and plunging into the Arabian Sea.

The next image caused a sharp inhale as Keir stared at an image of Radeeka and her parents sitting at their dinner table. There was an image of Ruchi serving dinner, wearing a lovely blue sari, Raj reading to Radeeka on the sofa, and another of all three posing with Lord Ganesh in the foyer of their flat just before he left that evening, the last time Keir saw Raj and Ruchi alive.

Keir remembered Raj's explanation of the Ganesh Festival, *At the end of the ten day festival, the idols are immersed in the sea to cleanse the water. The plaster of paris dissolves, reminding us that the universe is in a constant state of change. Sooner or later, form yields to formlessness, but our energy remains.*

chapter 28

LEARNING TO LOVE

Every evening, Claire came home from work mentally exhausted but she and Keir rarely spent a night apart. If Keir had the time, he stopped at the market and cooked dinner for them in her flat. If his schedule precluded the market and cooking, they ate dinner at the hotel restaurant and retreated to his suite and its clean, air-conditioned atmosphere.

Claire had been in India for over a year, but she still avoided the city streets beyond her office, her flat, and the ride to Bhojan Thali. After hectic days at work, she wanted to relax and be comfortable.

Keir presented her with the new camera and fifty rolls of film. He hoped to lure Claire out of her insular western comfort zone. "Shoot with abandon," he said. "Few cities on the planet offer the frenzied sensory stimulus of Mumbai."

"Thank you! I love photography. When I was five or six my parents bought me a Kodak Brownie. I even used flash bulbs. I carried it everywhere, pretending I was a journalist," she told Keir.

"I hope your mother saved your work, I'd love to see it."

"I'm sure she did. She meticulously recorded everything. Next time I'm home, I'll look for the photos." For just an instant, enduring the stab of sorrow, she wondered where she had hidden the photo albums of Lisa's short life.

They walked toward the hotel from Claire's flat. She wished the film could capture the scent of India: sweet tropical flowers and pungent spices mixed with human waste and decay. She photographed the leper and the man without hands who begged near her flat, and the ever-multiplying population of children who pleaded for a coin or food. She shot candid and powerful images; dirty little fingers tapping muddy lips, rags ineffectively protecting festering wounds. She photographed cows and water buffalo who claimed the streets and parking spaces as they roamed among auto rickshaws, buses, and taxis without restraint.

The zoom lens provided distance and anonymity. Claire discretely captured images of an old woman crouched in the street. Wet cow manure oozed between her fingers, splashed onto her sari, and speckled her naked breasts hanging like empty pockets. She had no *choli*. The foul -smelling woman arranged the disks like huge hamburger patties on the griddle-hot sidewalk, stacked the dried cakes against a stone wall and sold them for cooking fires.

With Keir's love and support, Claire allowed herself to truly feel empathetic and experience the sorrow passing on through her without being absorbed into her heart. For the first time she was able to venture further into the intriguing corners of Mumbai and began to see beyond the poverty and despair. She saw the richness and multiplicity of the city: Mercedes and ox carts sharing the street while cows roamed freely. Skyscrapers and cardboard shacks. Proud parents and children happy regardless of their life of abundance or lack. She realized that she never heard a parent scolding a child as she so often did at home in the states. She began to recognize herself as a complete person, more than the powerful and stoic business woman in charge of big projects but also a person who was able to understand and accept her own emotions. She wanted to get better acquainted with that part of her Self. Her love for Keir and Shakti, and their love for her cracked the wall that had safeguarded her from her true Self since 1971 when she lost Lisa.

Keir's new driver, Sunil, drove them to markets and neighborhoods not often visited by tourists. He discretely followed on foot assuring their safety, and remained available to answer their questions.

Palm lined boulevards lead to gated compounds surrounded by ten-foot brick walls. Broken glass protruded from the last layer of mortar, as effective as razor wire at discouraging intruders. Clustered between the mansion walls, squatters' slums seethed with daily life. Cooking, eating, bathing, defecating, copulating, all managed without privacy, without running water, and without soap.

She photographed doorways made of intricately carved wood, some with curling, faded paint that might have been in London or Paris. She captured a vine covered stone wall. An arch of flowering vines and the colonial mansion beyond caught her attention with its extravagant wrought iron gate featuring leopards and palm trees. She didn't notice at the time that the fancy old English script on the brass placard read *Achara*. They discovered sometime later that the property was owned by Mr. Achara from the adoption agency. The photo would mean a lot to Shakti in years to come.

Claire beckoned for Sunil to come closer, "What is that

lovely fragrance?" she asked.

"Madam, you are smelling passion flower. The fruit of this plant is delicious and the flower is beautiful. Hummingbirds are quite fond of passion flowers," said Sunil.

"You have an interest in plants?"

"Yes, ma'am. I hope to become a botanist and discover how to grow food for the poor."

Sunil took them to the furniture market where the strong sweet smell of wood filled each shop. Behind one store, Claire photographed a man sitting in the barren yard carving delicate cabinet doors from Sheesham wood. He used primitive hand-made tools secured by his three fingered hands as well as his toes.

In the middle of the crowded sidewalk, a potter turned his wheel. A river of rich, red, clay-water ran into the street. Terracotta dripped from his elbows, dried on his sunbaked skin and stained the bare feet of people passing by. Pots of all shapes and sizes, some delicately painted, some left natural, stood precariously stacked around him. Shoppers veered to avoid them. As Claire moved for a better shot, the apprentice encouraged Keir to buy baking dishes and water pots. "Very good for cooking. Very good for water. Please, have. Just for you, thirty rupees only." Knowing that the locals would pay three rupees, Keir offered fifteen, bartering for the sport; it was expected. Ultimately he paid twenty rupees, about half a British pound, for a round bottomed water pot. He had watched local women balancing such pots on their heads as they returned from the polluted river.

Bumping into an olfactory wall, they entered the spice market, trading the sour odor of human waste, exhaust fumes and rotting garbage for the zesty, sharp, and sweet aromas. Spice *wallahs*, both men and women, squatted in their tarp-covered stalls with their arms wrapped around fabric-covered knees. Big bowls like gold-miner's pans held row after row of cone-shaped mounds of powder in varying shades of yellow, red, blue, sage, and purple, each more intense than the last. Other bowls held stacks of chilies, turmeric, cumin, saffron, ginger, cinnamon, mustard and many delicacies neither Keir nor Claire could identify.

In a textile filled alley, Claire photographed a woman squatting in front of an upright loom. Her fingers nimbly danced over the warp, weaving a carpet of finely spun wool. A baby with long black eye lashes, plump legs and arms, and creamy dark skin, slept on her back, secured by a length of blue and yellow cotton fabric. Something in Claire ached to hold the baby, a new phenomenon she had been experiencing since meeting Shakti.

A naked, dust covered toddler squatted nearby. His dimpled little hands scooped dirt into a green plastic Sprite bottle. He poured the dirt into a mound, and scooped again.

Like a rainbow gone mad, the next row of shops burst with fabric in vibrant greens, iridescent yellows and luminous blues. "Come, sit, I show you beautifying silk only, good price for you, you looking good."

As the day progressed Claire ignored the dust that stung her eyes, the stench that irritated her nostrils, and the perspiration that trickled between her breasts. The camera helped her find a mental refuge inside herself where the pandemonium heightened her appreciation for life. Separate and secure, yet curiously one with the chaos, she held the camera before her, inspired rather than consumed.

Under another blue tarp, crystals covered a surprisingly clean, violet colored cloth, watched over by a light skinned Indian woman. The woman seemed to float above her treasures as her cobalt and gold sari hid the wooden stool beneath her. A thick black braid with flashes of silver fell over her shoulder and red *sindoor* powder blazed in the part of her hair. Her soft and subdued black eyes captivated Claire. "May I take your photo," asked Claire, presenting her camera.

With the slightest twist of her head, a perfect white grin and twinkling coal black eyes, the woman communicated her permission.

Claire bent to capture the best perspective and Keir stood back with the bag of lenses and film over his shoulder, assuring that his shadow fell out of Claire's frame. When she finished snapping, they knelt to investigate the display of crystals. Claire squeezed rose quartz in each palm, one a perfectly round sphere, the other a multifaceted formation. She examined the other crystals and rocks; transparent deep purple amethyst, golden yellow and pale purple ametrine, steely flakes of lithium, brilliant yellow-green stichtite, clusters of shu fa, and marbled sea-green fluorite. She tried but couldn't deny the energy that passed through her chest as she touched each stone.

In Hindi, the woman said, "The pink crystal has soft feminine energy of compassion and peace, tenderness and healing, nourishment and comfort. It speaks directly to your Heart chakra, dissolving emotional wounds, and reawakening your heart to its own freedom to love."

Claire smiled and nodded, feeling the words more than hearing them. "Do you know what she said?" she asked Keir.

He had enough Hindi to understand the spirit but not enough to translate. "Something about the essence of love and healing emotional wounds?" he shrugged. "She seems to know that rose quartz is ideal for you."

Claire smiled at the crystal *wallah*, tilted her head toward her camera, and paid more than the amount the woman wrote on a notepad. Claire smiled and nodded as the woman said, "Namaste."

Unusual fragrances lured them further into the shadowed alley to a shop that sold incense and oils. Keir watched Claire's face relax and soften as she hugged her bag of tissue wrapped crystals and breathed the discord of fragrance in the shop.

Keir had studied aroma therapy with a keen interest in the influences of fragrance. Sniffing each bottle, he selected body oils scented with sweet jasmine, flowery and stabilizing kewra and warm, calming sandalwood. He bought joss sticks, hand rolled with frankincense and patchouli and a wooden banana-like holder with holes drilled to secure the joss sticks while they burned.

Claire placed the bag of crystals, oils, and incense on the table next to her bed. "I'm taking a quick shower to rinse off the dust of the day," she said as her sun-dress collapsed to the floor.

"Can I join you?" He unbuttoned his shirt soaked with perspiration as she adjusted faucets on both sides of the two headed shower. They stood back to back enjoying the warm water. "I wish I could have photographed the look on Shakti's face the first time she stepped into warm, running water and smelled the soap," said Claire as she turned to let the warm water flow through her yellow hair. Keir bent to kiss her throat. "I'll never take a warm shower for granted ever again," she said.

"I agree," he said.

Claire turned off the water as Keir reached for a towel and asked, "Do you mind if I do my meditation in the sitting room? Maybe half an hour? Then I'll fix us something to eat."

"Of course, no worries," she kissed his warm shoulder. "I'll start on one of the books I brought from home that I haven't had time to read."

Keir disappeared into the living room as Claire unpacked the crystals, oils, and joss sticks.

Wrapped in a towel, Keir sat on a cushion on the floor and began to chant so quietly that Claire could only faintly hear from her bedroom.

Losing interest in the novel, Claire inspected the bamboo skewers coated with pungent powder, tentatively bringing one to her nose.

She lit a candle, always ready in case of a power outage. Borrowing its flame, she lit the incense, secured the other end in the wooden holder, and placed it on the dresser. Smoke twisted upward like a child's soft curls, diluting the sour scent that always lingered. She turned down the bed spread, exposing a crisp white sheet. Warm and humid air caressed her skin as she lay back on her pillow. The scent engulfed her. Light through the sheer curtains cast a dim violet glow throughout the bedroom. Her fine cotton nightgown merged with the smoking incense. The aroma aroused her. She sensed more than heard the muted pulsations of Keir's chant vibrating vivid notes like those of a wooden flute, na-mo, na-mo, na-mo.

As if responding to her, Keir moved to the bedroom, his towel dropping to the floor. From the doorway, he smiled, contemplating her flawless fair skin under the sheer violet nightgown, long pale lashes closed over her big eyes, wavy blond hair fanned on the pillow like the wing of a tropical bird.

Sensing his presence, she reached out without opening her eyes.

He opened the bottles of oil, stood by the bed and

wove his fingers with hers. With strong thumbs, he massaged jasmine-scented oil into her palm and each finger. Moving up her arms his gentle hands rubbed her throat with the rich relaxing kewra oil and its notes of sweet fruits, musk, and vanilla.

He climbed onto the bed, kneeling by her feet he lifted her leg and rested her foot on his hard belly. His thumbs rubbed saffron oil into her arch, each toe, and ankle. He added sandalwood oil to his warm hands and caressed her calves and shins. She gasped as his long fingers continued up her thighs and the powerful scent mingled with the smoky air.

He turned to sit near the edge of the bed, his feet stretched before him on the cool marble floor. She stood up on the bed with her feet on either side of his buttocks. She pulled her nightgown over her head and let it float to the floor. His oiled hands grasped her waist. Her knees bent, and she lowered herself as his palms guided her.

Still holding her waist, he rolled back onto the white sheet as Claire hovered over him, lifting and lowering her body until she fell forward onto his chest. They rolled together, onto her back, her legs wrapped around him like a snake, her feet locked behind his back like a golden clasp. After a surge of power, their tantric ritual subsided, each partner steeped in mindful awareness. Their passion rested while they hummed the chant together, na-mo, na-mo, na-mo, then ignited again, and again. The amethyst glow of sunrise through the curtains found them joined in harmonic satiety, ready for sleep at last.

🐘 🐘 🐘

As they drank coffee, Claire said, "What *was* that?"

"What do you mean?"

"I have never experienced anything like last night.

Not even close." She refilled their coffee cups and sat on the sofa next to him, comfortable in her own skin for the first time in her life. "I'd like to think it's because we love each other, but there's more to it. . . ."

"It was far more," said Keir, leaning forward, resting his elbows on his knees, and clutching his coffee mug with both hands. "We opened to a tantric experience. It had more to do with our mental approach to each other than love or technique. I knew that the oils would help prolong orgasm, but I had no idea. . ." He smiled and shook his head, staring into his coffee. "Extraordinary."

"It was as if I went to another place. My mind went quiet. . . . Don't take this the wrong way," she said as he turned to face her, "but it was as if you weren't here. I just floated away on the scent of the oil and the touch of your hands."

"No offense taken, I was out of body as well, detached from you and India and the craziness of our lives here. We merged in a place that is not of this planet. We were together but someplace else. . . parallel. The oils and massage helped us give ourselves to each other while our minds released. If you're thinking too much about sex and being turned on, you're only partly aroused. But if you just let go, something remarkable happens."

"I'll say! Can we do it again?" she said, rubbing his back.

"The question is, can we let it happen again?" he said, looking out the window, in a daze, drinking his coffee.

She put her coffee on the table, took his cup, and placed it next to hers.

"I've never felt so free in my life." The scent of sandalwood oil lingered on her skin as she pulled her nightgown over her head.

"Yes, of course, . . . Oh. . . You mean straightaway!"

chapter 29

THE WEDDING

Neither Ashook nor Neela had a birth-family and they shared parents; Chachi and Chacha. Planning a traditional Indian wedding was confusing at best.

For the event, Chacha took the role of Ashook's father and Chachi the responsibilities of Neela's mother. Chachi invited Claire to participate in the bridal preparations the day before the wedding.

Claire took time off from work to join them. Most of her new staff had been hired and training was underway, but delayed cell site construction prevented progress. She would not be missed.

Claire watched a young woman steam Neela's traditional Indian wedding dress, moving the wand up and down inches from the rich fabric. A wide band of crystal beading with metallic green and gold thread sparkled around the open work at the hem of the deep burgundy-red lehenga. The skirt would float around Neela like a swirling disk of silk. The same crystal beading and embroidery adorned the elbow-length sleeves of the *choli*. Red, green, and gold crystals covered the *dupatte* that would be draped over Neela's flower-filled hair and shoulders.

On a small table, Neela's wedding jewelry waited: beaded ankle bracelets, long gold earrings, and glass bracelets that would adorn Neela's arms below her elbow. "Chachi wore this jewelry at her wedding," Neela told Claire. "I didn't know until this week that Auntie and Uncle also have a love marriage. This will bring us good luck," she said, touching the sparking gold.

The mehndi artist arrived and began to decorate Neela's hands and feet with temporary henna tattoos. The smell of eucalyptus filled the room. "Neela, that's beautiful," said Claire. "What's the paint made of?"

"She uses henna paste she makes from crushed henna leaves mixed with eucalyptus oil, turmeric, lime juice, and black tea. This recipe will make the mehndi darker on my skin, and it will last longer than other recipes, but eventually it will wash away."

"Is the design symbolic?" asked Claire.

"Yes ma'am. The stars, sun, and moon design I chose symbolize the love Ashook and I have for each other." She smiled and lowered her gaze. Claire noticed that Neela's dark skin blushed when she spoke of Ashook.

"How long will the henna last—before it washes off? Oh, I hope I'm not asking too many questions."

"Not at all, I am pleased to answer. The henna will last longer than a month," said Neela, holding her hands for Claire could see. The delicate drawing twisted like dark chocolate frosting piped onto her skin.

Claire turned to the artist, Aruna, now starting to paint Chacha's hands. "You are a talented artist."

Neela translated.

Aruna smiled and lowered her chin.

Claire regarded her own pale hands, *my skin is pale, and lifeless compared to these beautiful women,* she thought.

"Would you like Aruna to paint your hands Claire? There is a book of designs you can choose from." Chachi nodded toward a notebook on the table.

"Yes, I think I would, very much," said Claire without hesitation. She leafed through the notebook and chose a simple but elegant design.

When the artist finished, the three women sat in the shade on the lawn while the henna paste dried.

"Do you know the meaning of the pattern you selected?" asked Chachi.

Claire shook her head, "No, I just like the art of it, not too heavy." She held up her hands and admired Aruna's fine work.

"The six pointed star signifies union of feminine and masculine principles," said Chachi. "This could mean within yourself. Many Western business women have strong masculine energy. The circles represent infinite wholeness and perfection," Chachi smiled, "I suspect you are a perfectionist at the office and perhaps elsewhere."

"Maybe a little. What about the ocean waves, I love how they move on my wrist."

"The waves symbolize deep passion and tantric ecstasy."

Claire blushed and turned away, embarrassed to reveal her recent experience with *tantric ecstasy.*

A delivery truck arrived with white tents, folding chairs and tables, potted plants, and boxes filled with marigold leis, and stems of stephanotis, jasmine, and freesia. Chachi began directing the delivery men while Claire and Neela retreated to the bride's quarters.

"Neela, I forgot to ask, how long until I can wash

my hands?" asked Claire, looking at her henna decorated palms.

"You can wash them now if you wish. The paste is dry and the stain is in your skin."

"That's good, I need to use the rest room," said Claire.

"Rest Room?" said Neela, her head tilted.

"The facility." Claire laughed. "Sorry, we use some odd phrases in my country."

When Claire came back, Chachi was opening a box of flowers. Freesia and jasmine fragrance filled the room. We will put these in Neela's hair tomorrow morning, as well as Shakti's, but they will stay in the refrigerator until morning. Chachi signaled for a girl to take the box to the kitchen.

"Come, let me show you the dress Shakti will wear."

"How beautiful," Claire gasped when she saw the miniature version of Neela's lehenga and *choli*. "Has Shakti seen this?" asked Claire, tracing the open work.

"Yes, she tried it on a few days ago," said Chachi. "She was overwhelmed. Now she's in the garden, practicing her role for the ceremony. Mr. and Mrs. Hamadani will attend with Radeeka. Shakti is thrilled."

"Thank you for letting me be a part of this beautiful occasion."

"It is an honor. Our family is quite untraditional. Chacha and I did not have children of our own but we are blessed with a collection of non-blood related souls who deeply care for each other. You and Keir are members of our eclectic family." She bowed her head, "Namaste."

"Namaste," Claire whispered for the first time since arriving in India, her henna painted palms pressed together, tears welling on her lashes. The greeting filled her mouth with softness and her heart with warmth. Her life had shifted and she knew it. She had begun to focus on who she *was* instead of the person she always *thought* she should be.

Radeeka and Shakti had a few minutes together before the ceremony began. They sat on a blanket under the mango tree. Shakti knelt slowly to avoid wrinkling her sparkling *lehenga*.

"Look," said Shakti jutting her lower jaw, exposing the hole where a tooth had been.

"I lost my first baby tooth when I was five," said Radeeka. "You must have been three years old when we met. Do you remember?"

"I remember no other life."

"One morning I woke up behind the fruit-*wallah's* cart, and there you were cuddled next to me like a baby doll. You were wearing a beautiful red dress, and looked so healthy and smelled so good, like you do now. I know your mother loved you very much." Radeeka put her hand in her pocket. "This barrette was in your hair. I wouldn't let Jamal sell it." She used both hands to present the small silver barrette to Shakti.

Shakti stood, clutching the barrette in her palm, "Please help me, I want to wear it for Neela's wedding."

Careful not to disturb the white flowers in Shakti's hair, Radeeka fastened the barrette beneath them. "You are as beautiful as the bride." She kissed Shakti on both cheeks, and hurried to join Mr. and Mrs. Hamadani.

The *baraat* procession danced through the gates with Ashook riding a white mare. He wore a glimmering red satin *kurta*, white pants, a beaded headdress, and had allowed his beard to grow for the occasion. The filly's costume shimmered

red and gold with flower garlands around her neck. Like brothers and cousins, the orphaned boys he'd grown up with danced around the horse with a troupe playing *dhol* and *tassa* drums, bells and symbols. Chacha held aloft an umbrella that matched the mare's brocade blanket.

Neela and Ashook stepped around the fire seven times, each reciting the Seven Vows of Saptapadi:

> Let us vow to nourish each other
> Let us vow to grow together in strength
> Let us vow to preserve our wealth
> Let us vow to share our joys and sorrows
> Let us vow to care for our children and parents
> Let us vow to be together forever
> Let us vow to remain lifelong friends

Ashook applied the red sindoor powder to Neela's hair and put the gold and black *mangalsutra* necklace around her neck. After Chacha tied their garments together, they kissed for the first time as husband and wife, then bowed to their guests.

The crystal beads on Neela's lehenga sparkled through Shakti's tears. Until wedding preparations began, Shakti had never considered the past or thought about the parents that abandoned her. For the first time, she longed for her own mother. *Why did my mother leave me in Radeeka's care?*

In a recurring dream, she played with her mother under an arch of passion flower vines, or was it a vague memory? The silver barrette begged her attention while the scent of the passion flowers mixed with the fragrance of the flowers in her hair. As her fingers rose to toy with the barrette, she imagined a yellow sari, unfurling and rising to join the moon's golden beams. In spite of the joyous occasion, a profound sadness punctured her happiness, *my mother had no choice, I am certain.* Shakti backed into the shadows and wiped her private tears.

Waiters dressed in white *lungi, kurtas* and marigold-colored turbans, lit torches around a temporary dance floor set up on the lawn under a big white tent near the passion vine trellis. Candles glimmered on every table.

At four stations chefs prepared food for guests, including curries, *samosas* filled with spiced vegetables, *pakoras* and a dessert display, with cake, *kulfi* and decorated sweets made from nuts.

Throughout the evening, Claire took the opportunity to meet Neela's university friends. She found them warm and friendly, *just as ambitious and eager to succeed as any young woman I know in the US*, she thought.

A musical ensemble dressed in orange turbans, *pajama kurtas*, and long Nehru vests, played traditional *tabla, sitar,* and *harmonium*. The music sounded like discord to Claire's ears as she watched men dance with men, women dance with women.

Later in the evening, another band took the stage, dressed in t-shirts and jeans. They played electric guitars and popular western tunes like "This Is Your Night", "All That She Wants", and "Whenever You're Near Me".

A machine began spewing white fog and laser beams pulsed over the crowd as the t-shirted band sang *The Macarena*.

> *Dale a tu cuerpo alegria Macarena*
> *Que tu cuerpo es pa' darle alegria y cosa buena*
> *Dale a tu cuerpo alegria, Macarena*
> *Hey. . . Macarena*

Everyone under thirty sprang to the dance floor. A blur of vibrant *saris, kurtas,* turbans, and western style clothing, women and men alike, formed a circle around Ashook and Neela. With all the hand movements and hip gyrations, they danced *The Macarena* in unison. Radeeka and Shakti stood nearby laughing as they shook their hips, mimicked the hand movements, and tried to sing along, "Hey, Macarena."

Chachi, Chacha, Keir, Claire and Mr. and Mrs. Hamadani watched with fascination.

"Just when I thought I had this country figured out. . . ," said Keir, shaking his head.

"Except for the costuming, we could be in Los Angeles," Claire added.

"I've never seen anything like it," said Mr. Hamadani.

While wedding guests ate and danced, Shakti led Radeeka into the house. Hand in hand, they stood, for no reason, by the open refrigerator, listening to the music out doors and smelling fresh fruits, vegetables and grains. Neither spoke.

They climbed the stairs and entered the bedroom. "Neela and I sleep here, but now, Neela will stay with Ashook," said Shakti in Hindi. "I am happy they love each other, but sad that Neela is going away to college in America."

They walked into the big room that was Shakti's school. Radeeka gasped, wide eyed.

"You do not have such a school where you stay?" asked Shakti.

"Shakti, I've never seen anything like this. This is your school?" Radeeka inspected the easels, with covered paint jars and clean brushes organized in crocks. She walked to the library corner and let her fingers dance from spine to spine. In the science corner she touched a microscope and a telescope. In the middle of the room a sandbox held red plastic buckets and shovels. Wooden boxes held blocks, Legos, toy trucks, and dolls. A pretend kitchen filled one corner with small wooden appliances, plastic plates, and miniature copper cooking pots. She walked to the windowless corner of the room. "This is an odd looking television," said Radeeka.

"That is a computer monitor. What is a tell-vision," said Shakti.

"Shakti, you know what a computer monitor is but you've never heard of a television?"

"There is so much to learn," Shakti shrugged.

"What is your favorite thing to study?" Radeeka asked Shakti.

"I like reading. I read books in Hindi then again in English. I also like maths, I learned to add, subtract, and multiply and now I'm learning fractions."

"You're doing fractions? Already? You've been here only a year. You've just lost your first baby tooth! I learned multiplication in third standard."

Shakti sat on one of the small chairs and Radeeka sat next to her. "Tell me about your school," said Shakti.

"We sat at desks in rows, listened to the teacher, and stood in a queue at lunch time. And we had to ask teacher's permission to use the facility," she said. "I haven't been back to school since. . ."

"Would you like to learn at my school? You could sleep in Neela's bed and we could learn together."

"Maybe I could sleep over for one night, but I couldn't leave Mr. and Mrs. Hamadani." She thought. . . *someday soon I'll have to start school again. Standing in queues, sitting like statues in rows, and asking permission at every turn, was absurd after living on the street.* "Would you like to come to my flat for a visit, and see where I stay?" said Radeeka. "I take a lift to my flat. I have my own bedroom with a bathroom. The maid cooks our meals and Mrs. Hamadani helps me with my studies."

"What is lift?" asked Shakti.

"It's also called an elevator. My flat is on the tenth floor, too many stairs to climb. So there is a tiny room attached to ropes and a motor and zoom, it lifts to the tenth floor!"

"I would like to see an el-va-tore, and I would like to visit where you stay," said Shakti. "Let's ask Claire and Keir to bring me there."

They ran outside. Claire and Keir, and Chachi and Chacha, were on the dance floor dancing to "The Way You Look Tonight". When the music stopped, Claire said, "I have never seen such a beautiful wedding. And Shakti, you are as beautiful as the bride."

"Yes, my dress is beautiful, just like Neela's, but tonight my room will be lonely without her."

Radeeka spoke to Mr. and Mrs. Hamadani, "Shakti has asked me to spend the night here with her, in Neela's place."

"We would love to have Radeeka spend the night with us," said Chachi. "I was planning to sleep with Shakti if she needed me. Radeeka is a better substitute for Neela."

"We have no objection if you're certain you want to," Mr. Hamadani told Radeeka.

"Can Shakti come to see my flat tomorrow?" asked Radeeka.

"I'll be their escort," offered Keir. "Sunil, my new driver, knows the way quite well."

"Oh, yes, I would like that, I have never seen a lift-elva-tore," said Shakti.

"You mean an elevator?" Keir smiled.

"Yes, Radeeka told me it lifts her to her flat many steps from the floor."

Keir sat on the chair next to Shakti, "Radeeka can stay here with you tonight, and tomorrow Sunil will drive us to Radeeka's flat so you can ride the elevator."

As the young adults partied, Chachi and Claire followed

Shakti and Radeeka toward the house. Shakti seemed to float above the grass wearing her long red lehenga. The beading sparkled in the torch light, and Radeeka's *salwar* outfit made her look older than her eleven years.

"Where will Neela and Ashook live in Seattle?" Claire asked Chachi.

"A friend of my husband has a house in an area called Tukwila. They'll take the bus to campus."

"Can I make a suggestion? My home in Seattle is within walking distance of the university and there's a furnished apartment in the carriage house. They wouldn't need to take a bus to campus, leaving more time for studying. If I contact the caretaker, she'll have the place cleaned and ready before they land in Seattle."

"That is very generous of you, Claire."

"It would make me happy to help them."

In the living room, Neela had left a small package for Shakti to find after the reception. White flowers and ribbon, like the ones in Neela's hair, secured homemade paper pressed with pink bougainvillea blossoms and tiny fern fronds. Shakti read the attached note aloud:

Dear Shakti,

I miss you already! It has been my joy to watch you grow in so many ways over the past year, and you helped me grow as well. Please write to me and tell me all the exciting things you are learning. I promise I will send you snaps of my school and our home in Seattle.

Much love,
Neela

With Radeeka, Claire, and Chachi watching, Shakti unwrapped the little package, careful not to tear the paper or break the flowers. Inside she found a barrette. On the back it said, To Shakti, with love from Ashook and Neela, May 10, 1998. She unhooked the barrette Radeeka had given her and handed it to Claire. Radeeka helped her clasp the new one and the two girls ran to look in the mirror.

Claire rolled the warm barrette over in her palm. "Auntie, what's written here?" showing Chachi the engraved letters on the back.

Chachi put on her glasses. "There is a date, 25 April 1972, and a name, Kala Seshan. Where did Shakti get this?"

"Radeeka said Shakti was wearing it the day they met on the street."

They stood looking at the barrette in Chachi's palm as if it would reveal its own story. "We must see what we can discover about this name, Kala Seshan." Chachi wrote the letters on two pieces of paper in both English and Hindi. She handed one to Claire and put the other in her pocket.

The next day, as Keir read the newspaper, Claire asked, "Do you remember reading something about the surname Seshan?"

"Actually, I do. That dreadful Atal Achara's dead wife was Kala Seshan." He heard her gasp. "Why? What? You look like you've seen a ghost."

"You know the silver barrette Shakti wore at the wedding? Chachi and I found engraving on the back." She handed him the piece of paper with the name and date in both languages. "Do you remember Achara's eyes?"

"Like Shakti's eyes, . . . but beastly."

The next morning, Sunil drove Keir to Bhojan Thali after dropping Claire at the office.

The girls were chasing a soccer ball with three other children until they saw the white car and ran to meet Keir in the portico.

"Keir, are you taking us to ride the ell-vatore," said Shakti, clapping her hands.

"Yes I am. Are you staying the night with Radeeka?"

Shakti's enthusiasm melted.

"One step at a time," he said. "You can decide after you ride the elevator."

"You will bring me back here after I ride the ell-vatore and see where Radeeka stays?"

"Of course. If you want to come home, I will bring you here, no worries"

"That is better," said Shakti. "I will decide later."

"We'll come home whenever you want. Are you ready to go?"

Chachi stepped into the sunshine. "They have been ready for hours," she laughed. "Please ring me if Shakti decides to spend the night with Radeeka."

"We will keep you informed," Keir said with a laugh. "I can't wait to watch Shakti ride an ell-vatore for the first time."

When they walked into the lobby, Mr. Hamadani hugged Radeeka. He turned to say hello to Shakti. "Nice to see you again. Right this way for an elevator ride."

He pushed the *up* button on the wall and the doors opened with a hum. Shakti jumped back two steps.

"Shakti, no need to be afraid. I've been riding this elevator every day. . ." Radeeka started to say *every day of my life*, but she didn't finish her sentence.

"Would you like me to hold you for the first ride?" asked Keir.

"Yes please," she said in a soft voice.

Keir hoisted Shakti onto his hip and they stepped inside. "I stay on the tenth floor," said Radeeka as she ceremoniously pressed the top button marked 10.

The doors closed and Shakti squealed with delight until the doors opened in front of the flat. Radeeka and Mr. Hamadani stepped off the elevator as Shakti said, "Can we do it again?"

"Sure! Can you push button number 0 to take us back down?" said Keir. Waving to Radeeka and Mr. Hamadani, "We'll be back in a few minutes."

Up and down they rode, until Keir finally put Shakti's feet on the floor in the flat next to the Ganesh statue. Next to it hung the large photo of Raj and Ruchi. A garland of dried marigolds hung from the frame, left from the memorial service that Radeeka had missed.

Radeeka led Shakti on a tour. "This is my bedroom," she said, "and this is my bathroom."

Shakti studied the western-style toilet and for no reason she understood, flushed it and watched the water swirl out and fill back up.

Her fingers touched the clothes hanging in Radeeka's closet; traditional Indian dresses, hanging among pastel cotton blouses, jeans, and pants. "You sleep here by yourself?" she said, touching the big bed.

Radeeka nodded.

They walked through the living room and into what had been her parent's bedroom.

While the girls wandered the flat, Keir and Mr. and Mrs. Hamadani chatted in the kitchen over a cup of tea. Keir pulled the envelope of photos from his pocket and slid them across the table. "I found an undeveloped roll of film in my camera bag," he said. "I had forgotten. . . ."

Mrs. Hamadani viewed the pictures, then occupied herself making tea. Mr. Hamadani also remained mute. Muffled street noise mixed with the ticking clock and whistling tea kettle as Keir respected their sorrow. The silence lasted several minutes.

"I had forgotten how much Radeeka resembles her papa. She looks so sweet in the shirt with the yellow kitten. It was her favorite," said Mrs. Hamadani, looking at the photo of the happy family. "When she came home, that shirt. . . ." She turned her back again, opened a cupboard, and put biscuits on a plate. "What those girls must have endured. . ." she said without looking at Keir.

In the bedroom, Shakti and Radeeka stood side by side looking out the window at the Arabian Sea. Shakti understood the depth of Radeeka's ordeal. "Tell me about your mama and papa," she said. "You must have loved them very much."

"Yes," said Radeeka. "Sometimes we had picnics on the beach. . . and Papa would read to me under a big umbrella. Mama made *samosas*. . . and *nankhatai*. Papa gave me coins for my pockets."

Once she started talking about her parents, the memories flooded back and she spoke with more delight, feeling their love as if they were in the room. "We dressed up and said puja at the temple of Ganesh every Tuesday, and walked to the orphanage so Papa could make a donation. That stone wall scared me when I was very little. I wouldn't put rupees in the basket, so Papa hugged me and told me how much he and Mama loved me."

It made Radeeka sad knowing that Shakti didn't remember her own parent's love. "Every day, after my bath Mama wrapped me in a towel. I tried to be grown up but she kissed my face and called me *My Sweet*. . . ." For a long time, they sat on the bed looking out at the sequin covered sea.

When they found the adults in the kitchen, Keir said, "Radeeka, I have something for you." His voice sounded grave as he handed her the envelope of photos.

Radeeka's legs melted and she sat on the floor. Shakti cuddled close to her as they studied each picture for several minutes.

"Where did you find these?" asked Radeeka. Keir could barely hear her.

"I left a roll of undeveloped film in my camera bag. I took most of them when I was here for dinner during the Ganesh Festival two years ago, just before the. . . the accident."

She wrinkled her brow, and squinted, trying to summon the memory of that night, only days before her parents died. "You knew Mama and Papa?"

"I worked with your papa at the university." Keir took a deep breath. "Radeeka, I wish I had recognized you on the street. . . but you were so thin, and. . . Oh Radeeka, I'm am so sorry. If I had recognized you right away. . . . I might have. . . ."

Radeeka unfolded from the floor to comfort Keir. "Please don't be sad uncle," she said, patting his shoulder, "I learned many lessons. Who would have cared for Shakti?"

chapter 30

TRUE IDENTITY

Keir had seen the unfinished exterior of Claire's office building but he had never been inside. At 4:00 pm he walked through what would eventually become the lobby, unable to wait any longer to tell Claire what he discovered.

Now he clearly understood why Claire went straight to the shower after work each day. The air was thick with construction dust and burned his eyes. A clothesline tossed with trousers, shirts, and men's underwear stretched near a rough concrete wall on one side of the huge room.

Julie, the tall exotic-looking vice president of customer service, stood next to a flip chart in front of the laundry training a group of new-hires while construction workers and their children milled about.

Keir easily found the door to Claire's office and closed it behind him. Her space was air conditioned, but he knew how hot it must get on the far-too-frequent days when the power failed. Still it was distinctly more pleasant than the rest of the building.

Clair looked up from her desk, holding her breath.

"Can I speak freely?" he said softly.

"Yes, Janus is out of the office for a few minutes, what did you find out?"

"There is no doubt, Mr. Achara's wife's name and birthday matched the engraving on Shakti's barrette. Achara must have assumed the girl drowned as well, or he just didn't care what happened to her. His infant son, Sanjay, is three years younger than Shakti. My assistant, Paku, speculated that the wife committed suicide when the family forced her to give up her daughter after the boy's birth. Apparently it's not uncommon for a family to give away unwanted female offspring."

"What did Paku learn about the daughter?"

"Her birth date was September 12, 1991, and her birth name is Devi."

Claire stood for a moment with her palms on her desk, absorbing the news.

Sunil drove them straight to Bhojan Thali.

🐘 🐘 🐘

"We must be very careful with this information," said Chacha. "Mr. Achara is powerful and could decide to make Shakti a maid in his household, or sell her. . . ."

"The Hague Adoption Convention was ratified a few years ago," added Chachi. "It states that every effort will be made to keep a child in the care of his or her family of origin. There is no mention of families who have discarded children like worthless toys. This could get complicated."

"Does your assistant know why you were curious, or that the girl is with us here?" asked Chacha.

"No. I told her we wanted to know all we could about Mr. Achara because Claire is interested in adopting. Paku assumed that the child drowned with the mother. Months ago she arranged for me to provide medical care for the nuns and internees at the orphanage but she's unaware of Shakti's rescue or our interest in adopting her, specifically," Keir said, putting his hand on Claire's shoulder.

"It is good that Paku is oblivious of the situation," said Chacha. "Perhaps it's best that no one else ever finds out, maybe even Shakti."

"She doesn't know her birth name or birth day," said Claire. "It doesn't seem right never telling her."

"I'll write a letter to her," said Keir, "to be opened when she's older, maybe 25? We should all sign it."

They agreed. Chachi poured brandy. They toasted, "To Shakti."

chapter 31

EDUCATION

As I learned reading, writing, and math at Bhojan Thali, Mr. and Mrs. Hamadani home-schooled Radeeka. After living for a year as a grown-up with responsibility for others, she found it impossible to become an elementary school student again.

Radeeka began spending weekends with me at Bhojan Thali. Soon she became a student there and returned home on weekends to be with Mr. and Mrs. Hamadani, while I enjoyed weekends with Claire and Keir. Sometimes we all flew kites on Chowpatty Beach, and had dinner together at Radeeka's flat.

When I was seven and Radeeka was twelve, we were free to study the subjects we were interested in, as long as we maintained focus on the basics, reading and math.

Once I went to the office with Claire and listened to her talk to engineers about cell sites and plans for the network launch. I understood some of what they discussed but I found it dry and uninteresting. However, when Keir brought me to the University, I found his work fascinating. I observed a surgery with his other students in the balcony above the operating theater and later listened to a lecture I didn't understand but loved all the same.

Radeeka noticed the contrast between the smell of the grounds at Bhojan Thali and the streets where we had lived, especially the lack of diesel fumes. She began to study how the buses, taxis, and scooters were powered. She read about alternative power sources, and how to power the vehicles without the smell and without the noise.

Meanwhile, I noticed the good health of our brothers and sisters at Bhojan Thali compared to children living on the street. On the street we suffered from dysentery and a constant runny nose. Minor wounds and sores healed slowly. I wanted to learn all I could about healing.

chapter 32

LAUNCH—2000

After more than four years, the telecommunications network was ready to launch thanks to Chacha's help.

During Neela and Ashook's reception, Chacha had suggested he and Claire meet to discuss the difficulties she faced closing cell site contracts.

A few days after the wedding, they met in the local partner's offices, with Jaydeep Pradant's and Chacha's attorney. The attorney confirmed that it was unlikely they would complete the project without offering some sort of "incentive" to property owners "outside the bounds of the contract."

"You know it's illegal for me to offer graft in any way," she told them.

"I think I have a way to make the arrangements perfectly legal from the perspective of the American company you work for while getting the contracts we need to move the project forward."

"That's fine gentleman," she said as she stood up. "Mr. Pardant, you have responsibility for closing cell site contracts." She pushed a stack of pages across the table. "Here is a list of owners and properties identified by the engineers. These properties will provide the coverage we'll need to launch the system."

She looked at her watch riding over the henna designs still dancing on her hands. "It's time for lunch, so I'll be leaving now. Have a lovely afternoon."

A few weeks later, Tom came into her office. "When I met with the land owners this week, they had all signed their contracts. We'll be building out cell sites at a frantic pace now that we've got the go ahead. How did you do that?"

Claire kept a straight face but her eyes danced. "I did nothing, really," she said. "I just gave responsibility for closing cell site contracts to Jaydeep. Let's be happy we got them and leave it at that. How soon do you think we can launch?"

"No more than three months. Let's plan the party and get our tickets outa here."

🐘 🐘 🐘

Claire and Jaydeep Pradant held a launch party and together cut the ceremonial ribbon while servants poured champagne and served *samosas*, *jalebi*, and *pakoras*.

Chacha and Chachi had planned to send a Baskins Robbins cake from the new store in Mumbai but anti-American protesters had burned down the building after President Clinton imposed sanctions because of nuclear testing in India and Pakistan. They sent a huge bouquet of tropical flowers instead.

Claire's assignment was complete.

🐘 🐘 🐘

After the launch celebration, Claire met with Jaydeep and offered to stay in India as a consultant working forty hours per month. That way she could renew her work visa and stay in-country until Shakti could leave with her. "I have experience in all aspects of the cellular industry, I can help manage special projects, research new equipment, or do customer service training if you need it. I have no desire to be in charge and pose no threat to your authority. In fact," she said with a grin, "I'm getting married and staying in India as long as it takes to adopt a child."

He was thrilled to have her stay on, and without thinking, gave her a hug. "Congratulations."

Keir's assignment had also come to a close so he proposed a similar arrangement at the university. He would stay on, teaching an advanced surgery class, in exchange for a work visa. Keir and Claire would spend the next four years in India, working toward changing India's international adoption laws.

🐘 🐘 🐘

After the monsoon, Keir and Claire held their wedding on the lawn at Bhojan Thali. Claire wore a sky-blue silk wedding *lehenga*, trimmed with crystal beads. She insisted Keir wear his jade green *pajama kurta*. The *Mehndi* artist painted Claire's hands and feet with henna in elaborate lace designs and Keir surprised Claire by riding in on a white horse. The ceremony, however, was western.

Two hundred guests attended from the university, the telecom project, and the hotel. Keir and Claire asked that donations be made to Bhojan Thali in lieu of wedding gifts.

Keir moved into Claire's flat where Shakti had a room of her own. Their expenses were no longer covered by their employers, but Claire had saved most of her per diem which gave them plenty of rupees to pay rent, and the cost of food was quite cheap compared to the US or England.

They still had to leave the country every ninety days to keep their work visas legal, so for their multiple honeymoons they took five day trips to places like Papua New Guinea, Nepal, Bali, and Fiji.

Their marriage, however, was not recognized by either the United States or England. They planned to make the marriage official in Seattle when Shakti could be with them.

chapter 33

SEATTLE—2004

Claire's head fell back as she savored fresh coffee with real cream, certain that the water used to brew it was safe to drink. Her caretaker had stocked the refrigerator with cream and fresh strawberries, and the pantry with coffee, Cheerios, tea, crackers and a loaf of artisan bread. Claire hadn't seen a slice of bread or beef since leaving Seattle.

There were no tiny hopping spiders or green lizards in the bathroom. The water pressure rinsed the shampoo from her hair and she didn't worry about getting sick if she opened her eyes or mouth in the shower.

The nape of her neck remained sweat-free as she walked to the kitchen.

She opened the windows to welcome fresh air that felt as clean as fresh squeezed lemon-juice. The house filled with the scent of late summer in Seattle; fresh cut grass, and hydrangeas, with no hint of human waste or exhaust fumes.

She poured cold, pasteurized and homogenized cow's milk over a bowl of crisp cheerios topped with sliced ripe strawberries, a breakfast she had longed for. She was tempted to make a roast beef sandwich to go with her Cheerios.

The grass was damp and clean under her bare feet as she walked to the dock. August sun warmed her back but the air was cool. She pulled her old terrycloth bathrobe closer. Robins kept her company in the otherwise silent morning. A great blue heron and his perfect reflection soundlessly stalked the water's edge as a raft of elegant mergansers swam above their own flickering likeness.

Standing at the end of the dock, she savored her mug of hot coffee, while pink pre-dawn light reflected on Lake Washington. *Sunrise is beautiful everywhere in the world,* she thought. She stretched to touch the water with her toe and watched the ripples distort the colors. *But I will never appreciate sunrise more than today.*

Keir joined her carrying a tray with a thermos of coffee, a pitcher of cream, a big bowl of strawberries, and a mug for himself. Over his arm he carried the pashmina wrap he had given her for her birthday. He draped the shawl over her shoulders and whispered, "Good morning, love," and bent to kiss her cheek.

She looked up into his eyes with a face covered in love and contentment. They sat in Adirondack chairs, enjoying the clean air, fresh scent, hot coffee with cream, and noiseless solitude.

She broke the silence. "Did you check on the girls before you came out?"

"Sound asleep. They didn't sleep a wink on the flight and they were so wound up when we got here, I hope they sleep past noon."

"I expect Neela and Ashook to be home around 5:00. Let's grill hamburgers for the girl's birthday celebration."

September 12th was Shakti's thirteenth birthday and Radeeka would be eighteen in a few days. Radeeka had grown into a beautiful young woman, taller than both her parents had been, with her father's intelligence and her mother's kindness. At thirteen, Shakti had reached her full height, just under five feet.

"I'm happy to help prepare dinner, but isn't Radeeka a vegetarian? Neela and Ashook as well?"

"I forgot, not everyone is starving for meat like me," she laughed. "I'll make Mediterranean pasta with tomatoes and feta cheese, but I'm having a hamburger. "

"Please, make one for me as well."

🐘 🐘 🐘

Sleepy-eyed, Radeeka and Shakti stood inside the house watching Keir and Claire enjoy the morning. Mesmerized by Lake Washington and the dock stretching into it, they walked barefoot, wrapped in blankets, past Keir and Claire toward the dock. No one spoke. They had seen photos of the yard and the dock but never dreamed they would be here together. The two girls sat down on the weathered boards and snuggled together under their blankets, Radeeka's arm resting on Shakti shoulders.

They had never seen mountains white with snow, a lake so vast and clean, or a great blue heron. They breathed the silence deep into their lungs.

🐘 🐘 🐘

A few days later, Keir and Claire were married in a quick ceremony on the lawn.

Keir's sister Adela and her husband Norbert attended the official wedding. Adela was a female version of Keir with chin-length strawberry blonde hair and a kind smile. Norbert was tall, thin and a little withdrawn, clearly a scientist.

They gave Keir and Claire a beautiful vase that once belonged to Keir's grandmother. Claire put it on the mantel where the cloisonné urn had stood for ten years holding her fathers ashes.

The next day they all visited the Space Needle, the Aquarium and toured Pike Place Market. Adela had her first latte at Starbucks and loved it. The girls enjoyed cinnamon rolls and marveled at the cleanliness of the city. "Where are the cows," asked Radeeka.

"They're safe in pastures on farms," laughed Claire. "Another day we will visit the cows."

Normally quite serious, Norbert laughed aloud while watching the fish mongers shout their order and toss the salmon over the counter, a Pike Place Fish Market attraction for tourists and locals alike.

Keir bought Claire a huge bouquet of flowers. Together they selected fresh vegetables, cheese, artisan bread, and potatoes to have with the salmon. That evening they all prepared dinner together. Radeeka, Neela, and Ashook loved the grilled salmon. For dessert, Neela and Ashook surprised Claire and Keir with a three-tier wedding cake from Hillcrest Bakery. It was covered with white marzipan decorated with chocolate cream piped into a *mehndi* pattern similar to the henna painted on Claire's hands at their wedding at Bhojan Thali.

chapter *34*

SHAKTI'S MUSIC—2002

In 2003 Radeeka and I took college entrance exams along with graduating students from Secondary Schools around Mumbai. She was seventeen, I was twelve. Our scores were very high. We both applied at University of Washington. By then, Radeeka had a passport but I thought I had little chance of acquiring one, much less a study visa, so we also applied to University of Pune and University of Mumbai. Imagine our delight when we were both accepted at University of Washington as well as Pune and Mumbai.

Chachi planned a Monday evening party, inviting Keir, Claire and Mr. and Mrs. Hamadani. The restaurant was closed as usual on Monday evening so everyone at Bhojan Thali attended. I thought we were celebrating our college acceptance letters. After dinner, Chacha gave a speech, congratulating Radeeka and me on being accepted into all of the colleges we applied to. Then he asked me to come stand with him. He presented me with a small package wrapped in beautiful homemade paper, decorated with red, white, and blue ribbon. Inside I found my passport and adoption papers, signed by Chachi, Chacha, Keir and Claire.

Keir, Claire, and I huddled in a hug for a long time while my friends and fellow students stood and clapped. Everyone cried, including Chacha.

Unbeknownst to me, Claire and Keir, with Chacha's connections, had spent hours each week for four years, vigilantly working to change foreign adoption laws so they could adopt me and take me to Seattle.

Keir, Claire, Radeeka, and I flew to Seattle in August so we could attend the University of Washington. Radeeka matriculated at eighteen, to study energy systems engineering. I enrolled in pre-med at age thirteen.

When I was a sophomore at University of Washington, I walked toward chemistry class one afternoon. I wore a UW Med Student baseball cap and my long ponytail swung over my backpack. I saw a cloud of kaleidoscopic colors, heard music, and felt my fingertips tingle. At first, I thought the music in my heart had grown loud, then I realized the sound came from a building. I dashed inside and followed the melody and the colorful cloud to the second floor where a tall, elegant woman, with silky blond hair and pale yellow dress stroked the strings of tall stringed instrument.

I sat on the floor next to her, forgetting about chemistry class. When she finished she said hello to me and saw my tears. "People often cry when I play Chopin's Fantasie Impromptu," she said. She asked if I played the harp.

I tried to explain, "I have never seen or heard of a harp but I have listened to this music all my life—in my heart," I stood to touch the harp's pillar. "Your music makes colors I have felt but never seen, until today"

Her name was Valerie. "I understand. I see the music too," she said. She looked at my hat, "The healing properties of harp music have been scientifically proven, I suspect healing is important to you as well." We had a long discussion about it. She told me, "One study showed that listening to harp can help regulate blood pressure, other studies show that head injuries heal more quickly when patients listen to harp music as part of their treatment. I will be giving a solo concert next week at Benaroya Hall. I have tickets for you and your parents if you would like to attend."

"Yes, I'd like that very much. Thank you."

Claire, Keir, and I sat in the front row. I longed to play like Valerie as I watched the colors flow, and felt the faint tingle in my fingers, as if I touched the strings.

When I enrolled in beginning music class and learned to read music a strange thing happened. I saw a distinct color for each note, similar to the way I saw the alphabet. The key of F was navy blue, C was bright red, and E flat was hunter green.

My piano teacher, Simone, also played the harp. One day she rolled it into her studio and removed the cover. It was almost a foot taller than me. She suggested I try it. I played an up and down glissando, and plucked a few notes to "Twinkle, Twinkle Little Star." When I looked up I saw tears in her eyes, "My dear, Shakti," she said in her French accent, "you have a natural musical talent, and a touch on the harp like I have never heard."

I had never before touched the strings of a harp. I saw the colors of the notes and tried to play with my heart fully engaged, as Valerie had played that amazing night at Benaroya Hall.

For Christmas, I gave Radeeka and Claire CDs of Valerie's harp recordings. I had no idea, of course, that Claire once played the harp. "I haven't played since I lost Lisa," she said. "You should have this." With a red big bow wrapped around it, Claire rolled her Lyon and Healy concert harp into the living room. It had been cleaned and tuned to perfection. The beautiful instrument was six feet tall and weighed seventy-eight pounds. Its tapered hard maple column had scalloped fluting and its soundboard was built with Sitka spruce.

2013

Ten years later, I still practice every day, study with Simone, and often play my harp's healing melodies for children in hospital. Although often taken for one of my patients because of my age and height, I am a practicing pediatric surgeon. I find that playing the harp is the most effective healing I can provide my young patients.

epilogue

2016

Keir and Claire invited Shakti, and Radeeka and her fiancé, to have dinner with them at the Palisade restaurant on Elliot Bay Marina. It was Shakti's twenty-fifth birthday and Radeeka's thirtieth. Neela and Ashook were surgeons at Swedish Hospital in Seattle, and owned a house on Magnolia, overlooking Puget Sound and the Olympic Mountains. They planned to join the birthday celebration after their baby's nap.

Radeeka and her fiancé had a flight to India scheduled for the following week. They were both teaching in the PhD program at Madras University, and had a grant to study the implementation of alternative power sources including solar and wind. As the middle class grew and automobiles became more ubiquitous in India, they hoped to leap frog the internal combustion engine by supporting the introduction of electric cars, similar to the way the wireless network Claire worked on surpassed the copper wires of POTS.

Keir, Shakti, and Claire, along with Neela and Ashook, had made plans to attend Radeeka's traditional Indian wedding at Bhojan Thali in Mumbai after the monsoon in 2017.

While they waited for Ashook and Neela, Keir ordered champagne and hors d'oeuvres and handed an envelope to Shakti. "It's time to share this with you. Would you mind reading aloud?"

In Keir's writing, the envelope read:

To be opened by Shakti on her 25th birthday.

The letter read:
1 June 1997

Dear Shakti,

Claire, Chacha, Chachi and I have agreed to keep the following information a secret until your 25th birthday.

At Neela and Ashook's wedding Claire discovered engraving on the barrette you were wearing when you joined Radeeka. It reads:

Kala Seshan, 25 April 1972

Careful research verified that Kala was the wife of Atal Achara. Kala drowned about the same time you joined Radeeka. We are certain that she was your mother and Atal Achara is your father. The name your mother chose for you was Devi. Your brother, Sanjay, was born on September 16, 1994, probably days before you joined Radeeka.

We suspect that Mr. Achara assumed you drowned with your mother. If he knew that you were alive he could make you work for him, he could place you in the orphanage, or sell you to— well, there are many things he has the power to do to his own five-year-old daughter. We are so afraid he will cause you harm.

You were born on September 12, 1991, the first day of the Ganesh Festival. We chose September 12 to celebrate your birthday, knowing it was your actual day of birth.

Claire and I met Mr. Achara in the Recognized Indian Placement Agency office when we were first trying to help you. Of course at that time, we had no idea he is your biological father. However we did notice his eyes are golden—although your eyes are far more beautiful.

One day when Claire and I were touring and photographing Mumbai, Claire snapped the enclosed image. We later discovered that it was your birthplace. The passion flower arch explains your affection for their perfume.

We all agree that it is best to keep your identity secret until you are older and safely out of the reach of Mr. Achara.

With all our love,

The letter was signed by Keir, Claire, Chacha, and Chachi.

Shakti paused, stunned, staring at the photo of a palatial mansion, her birthplace.

She slowly folded the letter then walked around the table to hug Keir and Claire.

There was a calmness in the room. A huge burden had been lifted. No one spoke. For a moment, they each relived their early years together, remembering horrors, terror, lose and love, each in their own way.

Finally, with tears flowing freely down her face, Shakti said, "Thank you for all you did for me. You encouraged me to be anything I was, or ever wanted to be, whether magic fairy or pediatrician." She laughed, "Good thing I chose pediatrics."

Keir took Shakti's hand and put his arm around Claire. "The bond between the two of you has impacted all of our lives. I am grateful to love and be loved by both of you."

The mood quickly changed to a celebration when Neela and Ashook joined them. Ashook carried three-year-old, Rajeesh, still sleepy eyed, and Neela held their four-month-old baby girl. As they settled Rajeesh into a high chair and Ashook took his seat, Claire indicated to the waiter that they were ready to order. "We have a surprise," she announced. The waiter brought a small Ganesh statue to their table.

"Radeeka and Shakti were both born during the Ganesh Festival. And I know how important Ganesh was to Radeeka and her parents." She smiled at Radeeka across the table. "This plaster of paris Ganesh has been on our dining room table for the past ten days. After dinner tonight, since this is the last day of the 2016 festival, we invite all of you to join Keir and me, as we celebrate Anant Chaturdashi and set the statue afloat on Puget Sound. If ever a family was given good fortune, it is our family." Claire pressed her palms together, "Namaste."

Glossary

Ayurveda: a 5,000-year-old system of natural healing that has
     its origins in India. Health is the balanced and dynamic
     integration between our environment, body, mind, and spirit.
     To learn more about Ayurvedic medicine visit
     http://www.chopra.com/our-services/ayurveda

Aham Prema, Ahan Prema: a. mantra meaning, I am love.
     See *mantra* below

achha: a versatile word with a number of meanings, including:
     I understand; Oh! Really?; Okay; Listen up, etc.

bab-la: food, often used by beggar's while tapping lips

bahut bahut: Hindi phrase meaning than you very much

bansuri: flute made of a hollow shaft of bamboo with six or seven
     finger holes

baraat: a bridegroom's wedding procession, it is customary for
     the bridegroom to travel to the wedding venue on a mare,
     accompanied by his family members

bhojan: (buhj-un) meal, food, eat grains

Bhojan Thali (buhj-un ta li) a fictitious estate in Mumbai, India,
     an orphanage for abandoned children. The facility houses
     a traditional southern style restaurant and open concept
     school.bindi: a decorative dot worn between the eyebrows by
     women in Indian.

challo: a Hindi expression meaning, *let's go*

chacha: Uncle

chachi: Aunt

choli (choh-lee): blouse in the Indian sari costume. The choli is cut
     to fit tightly to the body and has short sleeves and a low neck.
     The choli is cropped, allowing exposure of the midriff.

chromatic: 1. using musical notes not belonging to the diatonic scale
     of the key in which a passage is written. 2. produced by color.

clairsentient: phrase includes any or all types of psychic sensitivity
     corresponding to the senses: seeing, hearing, feeling,
     smelling, tasting, touching.

dhol: double-headed drum

dosa: fermented crepe or pancake made from rice batter and black lentils

duck: a British term of endearment

dupatte: length of material worn by women in India as a scarf or head covering, typically with a salwar outfit

expat: A person temporarily or permanently residing in a country other than that of their citizenship. Short for expatriate

harmonium: a musical instrument with hand bellows and keyboard similar to an accordion. It is used as an accompanying instruments in classical Hindustani music, Sufi music, bhajan singing, musical renditions of the classics and a variety of genres

hijab: headscarves worn by Muslim women. These scarves come in many colors and styles. The type most commonly worn in the West is a square scarf that covers the head and neck but leaves the face clear

idli: savory cake made by steaming a batter consisting of fermented black lentils and rice.

kurta: a dress-like garment for both men and women in India, worn over pants called pajamas

kulfi: Indian ice cream

lehenga: (leng-ga): long skirt, worn as the bottom portion of a Gagra choli or Langa Voni, popular for festivals and weddings.

lungi: white fabric tied like a sarong, then drawn up between his legs to look like pants.

mangalsutra necklace: necklace worn by married women in India

mantra: a chant during meditation that helps to induce an altered state of consciousness

mehndi: ancient traditional art of painting the hands, feet or body with a paste made from the powdered, dried leaves of the henna plant, cherry-red to brown color. For over five thousand years, henna has served as a symbol of good luck, health and sensuality. Mehdi in Indian tradition is typically applied during special Hindu weddings.

namaste: a greeting; "I bow to the divine in you." a respectful form of greeting, hello or good bye, similar to aloha, with palms touching.

paise: 1/100 of a rupee.

pakoras: fritters

pallu: loose end of sari, over shoulder

POTS: plain old telephone system

pranām: Hindi phrase meaning goodbye, respectful

puja: prayers

sage: one who lives "according to an ideal which transcends the everyday."

salwar kameez: a traditional Indian outfit.
salwar = pants,
kameez = dress or long shirt

shabdkosh: lemonade

shehnai, shahnai, shenai or mangal vadya : a musical instrument similar to the oboe, common in India. It is made of wood, with a double reed at one end and metal or wooden flared bell at the other end.

shudra: working or labor caste in India

sky burial: a human corpse is placed on a mountaintop or tower to decompose naturally or to be eaten by scavenging animals, especially vultures. Birds may eat it or nature may cause it to decompose. A generous or, in this case, inexpensive way to dispose of a corpse.

sindoor: a traditional red colored cosmetic powder worn by married women along the parting of their hair. Use of sindoor denotes that a woman is married in Hindu communities, and ceasing to wear it implies widowhood. The sindoor is first applied to the woman by her husband on the day of her wedding; this is called the Sindoor Daanam ceremony. After this, she applies it herself every day.

synesthesia: refers to a medical condition wherein one or many of
　　　　the sensory modalities become joined to one another in the
　　　　brain, giving color to musical notes, taste to a sound, smell to
　　　　a vision, or texture to an emotion.
　　　　https://www.psychologytoday.com/basics/synesthesia

Synesthetes can taste sounds, smell colors, or see scents, and
　　　　research proves these people —who make up 4 percent of the
　　　　population—experience reality differently.

tabla: percussion instrument (similar to bongos) a pair of hand
　　　　drums of contrasting sizes and timbres.

tassa drum: a form of kettle drum

thali: (ta lee) a round platter used to serve food.

upma: common South Indian breakfast dish, cooked as a thick
　　　　porridge from dry roasted semolina.

vada: fritter-type snack with origins in South India, served along
　　　　with a main course such as Dosa, or Idli. Best eaten while still
　　　　hot and crunchy, served with sambar, chutney or curd.

BIBLIOGRAPHY & RESOURCES

Synesthesia
   The Fascinating World of Blended Senses
   —Lyndsay Leatherdale

Wednesday Is Indigo Blue
   Discovering the Brain of Synesthesia
   —Richard E. Cytowic MD, David M. Eagleman PhD

The Frog Who Croaked Blue
   Synesthesia and the Mixing of the Senses
   —Jamie Ward

The Girl Who Heard Colors (children's book)
   —Marie Harris

Mirror Touch: Notes from a Doctor Who Can Feel Your Pain
   —Joel Salinas M.D.

www.apa.org/monitor/mar01/synesthesia.aspx

www.psychologytoday.com/basics/synesthesia

1. What was Kala's choice? Why?

2. Who was your most favorite character? Why?

3. Who was your least favorite character? Why?

4. Was the story believable? Why or Why not?

5. What other books did this remind you of?

6. If you were making a movie of this book, who would you cast?

7. After reading this book, would you like to visit India? Why or why Not?

8. What do you think the author's purpose was in writing this book? What ideas was she trying to convey?

9. What is original or unique about this book?

10. Share a favorite line from the book. Why did this line stand out?

Once a globe-trotting corporate executive, and long before that, a stay-at-home mom, Marcia Breece now lives on the Washington Coast where she has found her authentic Self.

Marcia's corporate career included working to establish wireless communication networks in India, Hong Kong, and Taiwan. In the 1990s, during her employment with AT&T Wireless, she worked in Pune, Goa, Mumbai, and Ahmedabad. In 1999, she returned to India for a three-month assignment for GTE helping to establish wireless and Internet service in Chandigarh, Punjab.

Writing first became her outlet in the late 70s when she began journaling. In the 80s she wrote user manuals and in the 90s she wrote articles for technical magazines but longed to write from her heart. After years of working in a corporate environment, Marcia realized she couldn't breathe deep enough and still show up at the office. A line from Mary Oliver's poem said it all . . . are you breathing just a little and calling it a life? ("Have You Ever Tried to Enter the Long Black Branches.")

She left her corporate career in 2005 to buy a llama farm and open a B&B. Her hens provided fresh eggs, the ducks, and geese ate the slugs in the garden and five llamas provided fiber that became beautiful rugs. As much as she loved the animals, she found that farm chores and tending to B&B guests left little time for writing. In 2011 she sold the farm and moved to the Washington coast where she lives with her two Havanaese, Dora and Ellie. "My wanderlust has passed. This is what I need for now."

When she's not writing, Marcia helps other authors self-publish their books, whether as eBook, POD, or audiobook. "It's a typical grass roots story," says Marcia. "An author friend asked me to help with his book, then his friend did the same, and soon I had a group of author clients that needed help with self-publishing. I'm convinced that if you stay open, what you love to do will find its way to you."

For more information visit
www.Publishing-Partners.com